# The Adventures of Ginger Mclean

**Amy Hodgins**

Fisher King Publishing

Cover design: Laura Thompson

Fisher King Publishing Ltd
The Studio
Arthington Lane
Pool-in-Wharfedale
LS21 1JZ
England
www.fisherkingpublishing.co.uk

For Tom, Jem and Ted

## Acknowledgments

Rick Armstrong at FKP (a jolly helpful chap who provides hope); Laura Thompson (illustrator and super sibling); Marion Francis (bloody kneed PE avoider); Geoff Cartledge; the Decedent Doughtys (Ben, Andrea, Dot and Sophie); the Marvellous Mays (Mum and Colin); the Hospitable Hodgins (Janet and Tim and the rest); the pupils and staff of Carr Manor Community School (especially 7B2 and 11S1, Ellen Johnson, Caitlin McDermott and Team PA).

To my extended social networking family (particularly you weird Facebookers and your sports day horror stories +53 likes); the pupils and parents of Kirkhamgate Primary School; Janet and Polly at Balne Lane Premier Stores; BBC Radio 2,3 and 4; Ted Snell (my own teacher of English) and of course, those forever on my mind: Mavis Cartledge, Arthur Doughty and Tony Doughty.

Last but not least... to Wakefield... you're cool... and I love you.

# July

*You are cordially invited to the…*

*Stanningate Year 6*

*'Moon and Stars' Prom*

*(Black Tie Event)*

*Friday 23$^{rd}$ July 6.30 – 9pm*


*RSVP*

*Mrs Lingaard*

*Tickets Cost £12 – meal included*

The invitation that landed on Ginger Mclean's desk was met with as much joy as a spelling test paper with a mark of 2/10. She lifted it reluctantly and stuffed it into her pencil case before getting on with the text message she was secretly sending Frances, who was sitting literally miles away at the back of the classroom. Should Mrs Lingaard discover that her star Year 6 pupil, the one *most* likely to receive a Nobel Prize, the one *most* likely to become a member of some national philharmonic orchestra, the one *least* likely to win X-Factor or ever have a boyfriend, was texting, she would have been desperately disappointed.

Ginger was not interested in the Prom for a number of reasons. For one, she was sulking because Mr Smyth, the head teacher, had written in her end of term report that 'Ginger is not a 29-year-old lawyer despite sometimes talking like one and would find making friends easier if she were to remember this next year.'

By way of punishment - for Mr Smyth having so little imagination - she would not attend his stupid disco. Everyone knew that a 'prom' was just a school party without the jelly, anyway.

What's more, she only had a couple of friends at Stanningate who she really would miss. She could picture the scene... everyone crying into their cokes and saying things like "I will miss you so much" and "it's the end of an era"... their tissues would be full of tears and there would be snot all over the dance floor... As if! All that gubbins after six years of arguing, pulling hair and calling one another names!

Nor was she in the least bit interested in wearing something that would be better suited to keeping a toilet roll warm. She had seen those girls on TV looking like Disney Channel rejects, unable to go for a wee because they had seventy-nine layers of netting under their dresses.

Finally, the idea of dancing in a public place to the *Cha-cha Slide* left the taste of sick in her mouth. Dancing, thought Ginger, was a very private hobby. What looked ace in your bedroom mirror and at dance class rarely looked so ace when you were sticking to spilt squash under a glitter-ball.

To summarise (a phrase Mrs Lingaard liked them to write at the end of their book reviews), Ginger would have rather had her tonsils taken out using her Dad's toe-nail clippers than attend the 'Moon and Stars' Prom.

Indeed, primary school had been a blast – a blast of cold wind on a rainy day in January when you've just come out of the swimming baths with wet hair.

It had started well enough: Ginger had been the star of the Foundation class and KS1, with her super-human literacy and mathematical skills. She could have been Super Times-Table Girl if she'd thought about it properly... got a costume and everything.

Back then, nobody cared about being popular, pretty or having the cutest little nose. It was all like, "Yeah, I can do number-bonds, what of it?" Filling up her chart with stickers from impressed teachers was the greatest pressure, being a 'teacher's pet' the giddy prize. However, since around Year 4, it wasn't enough to be great at lessons -

other stuff had started to matter too... For instance, hair seemed to occupy 80% of her school mates' minds. Ginger's was thick, brown and curly (not actually ginger, at any rate) - a source of much stress for her mother each morning. She woke up every day looking like she'd been electrocuted in her sleep. A regime of seven o'clock hair-pulling and taming it into a tight bun or French plait had not done any good for her mood each day. It was like being expected to sit quietly after a wild bear-fight.

Anyway, plaits had stopped being acceptable in Year 5 and since then it was all straighteners and extensions... beach hair and soft curls... Beach hair? Perhaps if it was okay to look as though you had just washed up on a beach after hanging to a raft in a storm for three weeks.

Somehow, even Ginger's face didn't match-up with what she believed was acceptable amongst eleven-year-old girls. Her nose was long and straight, not upturned and koala like. Her lips were full and pouty, handy for chewing on when she dealt with long division, but totally different to everyone else's. Her eyes were big and brown, but slightly sticky-out, like those bugs on the Discovery Channel. Also, being tall and skinny, there was no issue of bras on the horizon to occupy her on a Saturday afternoon.

Bras! That's all anyone talked about these days!

Personality was all about what you were *into* in Year 6. Were you *into* One Direction? Were you *into* boys? Were you *into* hair and make-up? Were you *into* dance classes? Were you INTO getting a grip and doing your own thing? Sheep! All of them.

Nobody else seemed to be *into* playing their cello, reading Percy Jackson books, looking at the *real* fashion in the *real* magazines or talking to Trevor about the meaning of life.

If it wasn't for Trevor and Frances, Ginger thought she might be very lonely. Trevor was Ginger's girl-hamster. Trevor had not been recognised as a girl hamster before the naming ceremony had taken place and Ginger, at the tender age of nine, hadn't seen any good reason to pick out a more feminine name. "Trevor it is then!" Dad had said, putting down the hamster-care book which had clear diagrams for identifying the sex of furry rodents. Ginger wasn't sure but she thought that Trevor might have rolled her eyes...

Absolutely the best thing about Trevor was how patiently she listened, never offering a stupid opinion. Frances was much the same and it was a solid basis for any friendship.

Being truly original was a poison chalice. It was often mistaken for being disagreeable. It was by the skin of her teeth that Ginger hadn't been sent to see the lady who came in once a week to talk to the kids with special problems, like divorced parents or unhealthy internet habits. She supposed Percy Jackson was one of those special kids. It could be cool to be different but then Percy didn't have to go to Stanningate Primary School with Stephanie Sykes.

Every now and then Ginger wondered if she was a scout from another deeply superior planet, sent to earth to investigate human society and that one day, she would receive contact from others like her... others with highly developed intelligence in little leopard print space suits…

Leopard print. It was her theme.

The one blessing at Stanningate was that the uniform was strict enough to give her and her friends little to worry about when the alarm clock went off. However, the other girls still managed to transform the burgundy sweat-shirt and black trousers or skirt into something that Barbie might wear. Ginger had more respect for the rules, but liked to quietly accessorise with something she had learned about in her older sister's *Grazia* magazine. Ginger loved fashion, as an expression of something more than how inappropriately sexy she could look. Gross. Today, she had thrown a leopard print scarf on (obviously) and was quite pleased with the result. This happened to match her leopard print rucksack and socks, but not her pencil case as that might have been overkill. She had long come to realise that her little creative touches were unappreciated by her school peers; she often got called 'emo' and 'mosher', but Ginger remained true to her style and resigned herself to the fact that being 5'7" at eleven-years-old, she was going to stand out at high school anyway.

She guessed that most of the other Year 6s were scared about High School and were using the prom as a distraction strategy, despite their bravado. They'd all heard the stories of what happens to Year 7s. None of it was good. Gone would be the cosy story times or crying when you tripped playing in the playground. However, it would be the beginning of a new phase for Ginger - she had decided - a chance to recreate herself; a chance to meet new people who wouldn't remember the terrible incident on the school trip to the Yorkshire Dales when Ginger had got stuck in worm hole of a cave and freaked out. Or when she had 'lost' her skirt after games in Year 5 and had to wander around in her yellow 'Thursday' pants trying to find it before being given some tight Year 2 shorts to wear.

Ginger had never swallowed the 'lost story'. She had never 'lost' anything in her life. She knew that the skirt had been hidden in the caretaker's cupboard by someone with pink glitter on their fingers... And it didn't take a TV detective to work out who always had pink glitter on their fingers by first break...

Biting her lip with anger, she tried to focus on High School. 'Atherton Academy', it was called. Before, it had been called 'Stumpmount High'. Someone hadn't liked the name when the new people took over so they had given it a less weird sounding name and a new logo.

Whatever it was called, she and Frances would finally get to meet like-minded people who didn't think it was acceptable to wear leg warmers for PE lessons.

Possibly, she'd even meet up with some others from the spaceship she'd been dropped from...

Looking back down at the invitation that was just nudging its way out of the pencil case, as though it had a life of its own, she pondered briefly to herself. It wasn't that Ginger had no romantic ideas about proms and all those other American ideas that annoyed her Dad. Watching old teen movies from the DVD shelf in the living room had taught Ginger all she needed to know about how great it can be when an ugly duckling turns into a swan for that one special night. If there had been any chance that the Stanningate Primary Prom would live up to that kind of promise, Ginger would have been the first to buy a quirky dress and try out a new hair style. She might even break out some lip-gloss! But, it wouldn't be like that, would it? People's mouths wouldn't be all 'OMG!' when she entered the spangled school hall that smelled a bit of old biscuit and older vomit. SHE wouldn't show up all the mean girls. SHE wouldn't sweep Milo Costigan off his Converse. However, SHE most probably would be humiliated and lonely and that was all there was to it. Leave the expensive limo hire to the stupid pretty girls who wanted to be Katie Price when they grew up!

So, July came and went and Ginger didn't go to the Year 6 'Moon and Stars' Prom. Her parents told her she might regret it. Frances hid it well, but was obviously heart-broken not to be able to share the night with her best friend. Ginger Mclean had long ago decided that enough was enough and her goodbye to primary education would be a casual "see-ya" at the gates and a perhaps a hug for Miss Lingaard.

# August

Frances agreed to take care of Ginger's hamster, Trevor, for most of August, whilst Ginger and the rest of the Mcleans hit France in the Volvo.

They had met the evening before the big drive to Calais, Frances weighed down with a photo album and a ton of gossip from the prom. She had taken it well that her best friend hadn't been there to share it with her and spilled the beans on all the totally embarrassing bits that she knew Ginger would like to hear about. Not once did she tell Ginger that it had been one of the most fun nights of her life but that she had cried a little bit because she hadn't shared it with Ginger.

After saying goodbye to Frances, Ginger tried to look forward to the holiday.

Most awesomely, Alex, her nineteen-year-old sister and Adam, her seventeen-year-old brother, honoured the family with their presence. It had been years since they had all been together for so long and incredibly, everyone got along.

Mostly.

Even her Mum and Dad managed to relax and have a sense of humour, often distracted from getting on Ginger's case by Alex and her daring bikini choices.

Mostly.

The last couple of years had been tough in the Mclean household. Mum and Dad hadn't been getting along for years but recently, they seemed to live separate lives, only coming together for family holidays. They passed on the stairs without a word to each other and Ginger had noticed that Dad often slept on the sofa because 'of his snoring' (said Mum).

Ginger wasn't a fool. She sensed that there was more to it.

So when Alex, who had just finished her first year at university, announced that she fancied a free holiday, Ginger had literally jumped for joy. Alex always had advice on friendships, fashion and even boys, though Ginger had never actually got to try any of it out. Alex studied English Literature and thought of herself as some kind of expert on human nature. English Literature was the study of stories, poems and plays from all different times in history. She didn't think Alex had ever mentioned reading any Percy Jackson there but she did throw names around like Shakespeare, Woolf and Shelley. How amazing would it be to be called 'Woolf'? It would even make the name 'Ginger' sound less geeky.

Sometimes, Alex would tell Ginger about why a book was good, and even lend her the odd one to read. Usually, they were really hard to get into, but sometimes, they were worth the effort. *Frankenstein* had been surprisingly sad and another called *Northanger Abbey* had been quite spooky. Mrs Lingaard seemed pleased when Ginger told her about them in her book reviews.

Ginger wondered what Alex had been like at Primary School, thinking there was no way that Alex could have been a geek or an outcast. This was something that made Alex laugh as she said that everyone feels like a nerdy loser between the ages of 10 and 18 - even the supposedly popular kids.

And so, they'd spent the summer laughing at Adam's attempts to impress the French girls with his boogie boarding in Biarritz, a place chock full of good-looking people and "too expensive" drinks (according to Dad).

Biarritz turned out to be a place on the Southern Western Atlantic coast of France and was pretty 'chic', apparently - a word Ginger's Mum often used to describe places that were dull and pricey. It may have been 'chic' for people who stayed in the big fancy hotels with pools and waiters, but not so much on the camp site the Mclean's were holed up in. More cheap than chic. Even sharing an igloo tent with Alex and consequently her make-up and accessories couldn't make up for the horror of camping, her Dad on his guitar and her Mum in her camping clothes which she'd been getting out every summer since 1985. It would have been completely unbearable were it not for Alex and Adam to laugh with. Safety in numbers was always best when taking the mickey out of parents:

"Mum, you look like a woman out of that show."

"Really, Adam? I don't think I want to know but which one?" she'd responded apprehensively.

"Doctor Who," he replied, not even looking up from his Kindle.

"You mean I look like his assistant? The pretty one?"

"No! The one that turns out to be a giant slime monster under her human suit. "

"She could pass for Simon Cowell in those trousers," added Alex, who was sitting on a picnic rug reading something called *The Colour Purple*.

"What do you mean, young lady? I've been wearing these for years and nobody's ever said I look like Simon Cowell. Are they too tight?" Mum started to rearrange her clothes, pulling bits up, bits down.

"Not if you were thinner, Mum, no," concluded Adam before closing his Kindle and wandering back into the tent.

Mum took it all in good-spirit. She was on holiday after all.

And so on it went.

Whatever Mum wore it was never as embarrassing as Dad in his tiny cut-off denim shorts and vest tops.

Worse, Dad would inevitably get his guitar out by the end of the fortnight (a project they'd been working on preventing for years):

*"Are you going to Scarborough Fair...Parsley...?"* he sang, pulling a face which Ginger thought was probably his best rock-star impression.

Adam looked up: "Parsley? Alex, Dad knows songs about parsley."

Their Dad stopped strumming and looked tight lipped.

Alex put down her book and pondered Adam's observation before saying: "Yes, Adam, but it's also about sage, rosemary and thyme."

"Dad, do you know any songs about oregano?" asked Adam.

"No. I don't. *Remember me to one who lives the-e-re...*"

"How about other vegetables?"

Looking exasperated, Dad answered. "They're herbs,

Adam. Gherkins are vegetables."

"Oh, my mistake," acknowledged Adam. "Do you know any songs about gherkins, Dad?"

It took about thirteen attempts and just about their Dad's entire repertoire of songs, but the children made the crooning stop in the end. However, Dad wasn't above taking his revenge:

"Adam, I can hear the noise coming from that iPod which means it is too loud and damaging your ears. Turn it down or turn it off!"

No response.

"Adam, can you hear me? Turn it DOWN!"

(Dad waving arms around like air traffic control and pointing at his ears).

Finally Adam responded: "What, you want to borrow some ear muffs? Ask Mum, she's got them in the medical bag."

"No, I want you to turn that rubbish off. What is it?"

"The Fur Blend. They rock!" replied Adam, banging his head up and down in time to the drums. "The NME say they're going to win the Mercury Music Prize."

"You know, they remind me of that group I like..."

A look of terror spread across Adam's sun burnt face... "I'm turning it off Dad. It's OFF!"

The only major problem with her parents (which led to a two day stand-off when neither of them spoke to each other) hit when the family were stuck in the Volvo on a day trip inland. The scenery flew by in a haze of broad brown, yellow and green fields and forest, foothills of mountains pointing to an indigo sky. Whilst the location was undeniably dramatic and picturesque, the atmosphere inside the vehicle was thick with the smelly cheese hopelessly contained in a cool box and a strange tension between the adults. Stopping off at a picnic area brought less relief than expected.

Dad drank too much with his camembert sandwich and announced that he didn't fancy driving back. "You'll have to do it, Annabel," he slurred, woozy with red wine and the heat.

"I'll drive, Dad!" offered Adam, who was about ninety-five lessons short of passing his driving test.

"No you won't, Adam," exclaimed her Mum, looking like she was going to cry. "Dave, you are totally irresponsible. Three children and a wife and you think of nobody but yourself."

"That's exactly why a man needs a drink!" blasted Dad before sitting himself back down on the picnic table at the side of the winding mountain road and uncorking another bottle of red wine.

It wasn't like him to be so cruel and self-centred, thought Ginger. He always drank too much, but he rarely showed anything but his embarrassing side. There seemed to be something more to it.

Silence between the pair of them followed for about two days. Being used to this sort of thing, Ginger, Alex and Adam did their best to ignore them and went about the business of making the best of the holiday. Nobody mentioned the elephant in the room.

But easily the most memorable bit of the holiday was not the long golden beaches, her parents' cold front or borrowing Alex's clothes; it was stopping at the motorway services at Watford Gap on the long drive home.

Standing in line for the toilet behind 4,000 pensioners on their way back from a trip to Windsor, Ginger felt *that* desperate that she was considering using the bin in the doorway to wee in.

Having run out of books about two weeks earlier, she tried to focus on the article she was reading from some rubbish girls' magazine she had found to read in the shop.

*Dear Bryony,*

*I have a big crush on a boy at my school. He is really popular and sporty. I suffer from obesity and feel bad about myself. The boy doesn't know I exist. How can I make him feel the same way? Please help!*

*Elizabeth, age 13, Leeds*

*Dear Bryony,*

*Some girls at school said I smell and have told all the boys. Now everyone is laughing at me and calling me names! I can't afford expensive deodorant and perfume because my parents are not well-off. How can I stop smelling bad? Please help!*

*Amy, age 12, Exeter*

*Dear Bryony,* thought Ginger, *I'm too tall, my parents hate each other and everyone thinks I'm a geek. Sometimes it feels as though nobody appreciates my amazing style and intelligence. And I really need the toilet. Please help!*

Then, suddenly, a voice that was oddly familiar drifted across from the arcade games on her left. It couldn't be, thought Ginger, as she tried to get a better view of the snowboarding game and the boys' heads that faced it, without drawing any attention to herself. Inevitably, the queue moved forwards at that moment and as she hurried to keep her place, she bumped into the old lady in front of her who was so old and frail that she fell like a domino and spilled her latte on the other old lady in front. This caused a stir amongst the old folk as they began to argue and use words unbecoming of the elderly in raised voices.

Staring carefully at a bit of chewing gum on the floor, Ginger sensed the boys at the arcade game turn to see what was going on and then, "Ginger Mclean? Is that you?"

Looking her in the eye, in all his surfy blonde glory, was Milo Costigan: star of the Junior Youth Orchestra, star of the football team, star of the Inter-School Quiz Team and love of her life...

The first thing that occurred to Ginger was that he knew her name, and her full name at that! The second was 'why now?' as, although she had also been on the Inter-School Quiz Team (and the source of the final winning answer), he had NEVER spoken to her before. Torn between pretending to be a foreign exchange student (she was tall enough to pass for a Year 9) and reaching out to kiss him in a very Year 4 sort of way, Ginger finally opened her mouth:

"Oh hi, Milo. It is Milo, isn't it?"

"Huh, yes, of course it's Milo, you doofus. What are you doing here?"

"Ah, well..." Ginger thought quickly, grasping for some cool explanation. It didn't come. "Actually, I need a wee. Really badly."

After that, all Ginger can remember is feeling dizzy and hearing a distant chuckle and something that sounded exactly like 'Ginger Mclean, you are such a weirdo.'

# September

'C YA IN 10. LUK LIKE A DWEEB. LOL' texted Frances, from five doors down the street. Ginger answered with 'ME 2. LOL' and put her new phone in her over-stuffed red school bag.

Ginger tried hard not to use text-speak in text messages. She thought it gave further ammunition for adults to mock young people. She used it begrudgingly when she had to, but wasn't able to help herself from exclaiming the odd 'OMG' in moments of crisis.

She had waited years for this day to come and here she was, looking the least cool she had ever looked in her life. Ginger stood a few metres away from the full length mirror to get a full view of herself in her uniform; the reflection did not please her. The blazer was too short in the body and too big on her shoulders, giving her the look of a gangster from a black and white film. Her hair had begun a revolution of its own, trying to sabotage any hopes she had of fitting in on probably the most important day of her young life so far. Panic had begun to strike at around 3am when little anxieties had prevented her from getting some much desired beauty sleep. Trevor had been at it in the exercise wheel for about two hours solid, showing no sympathy for her owner's nocturnal sleeping habits.

One source of the stress was the whole 'Ginger' issue. There would be the usual questions and sniggering. Her parents had clearly been drunk when making a name choice: "We just fancied something a bit different, sweetheart. Everyone is called Alice and Jessica; we knew you'd be special and you needed a special name!"

"Really? It didn't occur to you that it would bring me misery, bullying and a good reason to call the NSPCC to talk about child abuse?" Ginger had retorted in the kitchen over Chicken Kievs one Friday night.

"Ah, love. It's beautiful. Like the dancer, Ginger Rogers. Your Gran loved her."

And there was no arguing with Mum then, when Gran had been brought into the argument. Her name came up again now as her parents clamoured to take photos. "She'd be so proud to see you all grown up and heading off to get 25 GCSEs."

"I won't be doing GCSEs for a while, Mum. I have to get my head flushed down the toilet first."

Finally, Mum became bored of hanging around and went off to get herself ready for her work as a social worker. Dad left for his job at the local 6th form college, teaching Geography, after some furtive text message sending.

Just as the tears began to well up in Ginger's eyes, the doorbell rang and Frances fell into the hallway, looking a bit bundled up. She looked rather like a donkey in a new winter coat, its own blazer, plus at least three miscellaneous carrier bags and a violin. Never mind, thought Ginger, one of her Gran's favourite sayings was "be prepared for eventuality".

"As if," said Frances, doing a kind of curtsy whilst pointing to each aspect of her appearance she was unhappy with. In all fairness, even her truest friend couldn't deny there were a few teething troubles with this uniform malarkey. Frances looked as short and stubby as Ginger looked gangly and skinny - the stiff, ill-fitting uniforms only adding to the cruelty of their awkwardness.

Their friendship had been the most reliable aspect of their lives so far and this new challenge could be met as long as they met it together. Ginger looked at her best friend and thought that anyone who didn't have a Frances in their life was missing out. They had been inseparable since nursery. There they had enjoyed playing such classic games as 'Mummy's job' and 'Princesses get chased by witch'. Later, they had found that they had different interests but still the friendship continued. They would do their own thing when they were apart; Ginger had her music and books, Frances liked dogs, church and briefly, *My Little Pony*. When they were together, they looked at fashion and gossiped and every now and then still played 'Princesses get chased by witch', a secret that they would take to the grave.

"Come on, Franny, we can do this," consoled Ginger, not believing a word that came out of her own mouth.

The walk to Atherton Academy was about a mile, and it was not far enough that morning for the friends, despite the heavy loads of PE kit, pencil cases, violin and of course the cello. Registration was at 8.30, they'd set off in good time. Neither spoke much, apart from to deal with mundane communications about form teacher names and the offer of a Polo mint. The snake of students wound its way through the local estates and across a large playing field that looked like it needed a long drink after the dry summer. Men were working on replacing the athletics lines with winter sports ones. Most kids chatted, some pushed around, and older ones shared cigarettes. All of them looked much more confident than Ginger and Frances. Still, in the back of Ginger's mind there was still a glimmer of hope that this would be her time to shine; people would recognise her for being smart, highly fashionable and, eventually, popularity would come her way. Of course, she wouldn't want to be popular in that obvious way - she saw herself as more of a trendsetter, someone who was a bit different from the rest: mysterious and funny.

The girls arrived, sweating heavily from their heavy loads of PE kit and giant pencil cases containing the contents of an entire WH Smiths' store and were herded into the main school hall. They were instructed to sit on the floor by Mr Pearson, their Head of Year, and await further instruction. The instruction came as a kind of 'pep' talk; Mr Pearson clearly thought he was very funny and indeed, there was something clown-like about him: short, big shoes, over-sized lips and badly dyed hair. The pep talk worried Ginger; she had seen them happen in films. Usually, they were only necessary when a team had no chance of winning. This was not a good sign. He went on to describe the outline for the day. After they had been put into forms, they would spend the day doing a series of 'fun' team-building activities.

Ginger's upper lip quivered. There was no place in her life for team-building. She had come to see herself as a lone-wolf, just fighting for survival and possibly willing to kill if it meant she got to the deer-meat first (or the top score on a school project).

One activity stood out as being potentially disastrous. "Den-building!" announced Pearson, clapping his hands like a deranged seal at the brilliance of his own idea. Indeed, he got the reaction he hoped for as small boys everywhere punched the air in excitement.

Not so much Ginger and Frances.

Had Mr Pearson had access to Ginger's secret diary, he would have known that den building did not feature on her 'to do' list.

Ginger wondered if his feet were as big as his shoes or if they were real clown shoes and were full of padding.

They were joined by a girl called Rebecca, who Frances knew from a church youth club. Rebecca looked even more terrified than Ginger and Frances and had the tell-tale signs of tears around her small green eyes. Ginger gripped her hand. Even though she hardly knew Rebecca, she wanted to show her that she wasn't alone. "Don't worry. It'll be fine," she mouthed.

Scanning the hall for potential kindred spirits, Ginger noticed that almost everyone looked a little swamped under their too-big uniforms and even the Barbie girls from primary school appeared harmless.

As their names were called out and they drifted into forms, Ginger said goodbye to Frances, whispering "See you at break!" before joining her form tutor at the front of the hall. A pain stabbed at her chest a she watched her BFF wander away looking typically confused. Frances always looked a little confused. It was as though everything was a surprise to her. On this occasion she looked like she had just witnessed a bunny being squashed by a lorry. Ginger's heart went out to her. Could Frances make it on her own? Would she be strong enough without Ginger to hold her hand?

There was no time to formulate a plan about why they shouldn't be separated. Ginger looked around her to see how much worse it could get. Immediately to her right she found another unfeasibly tall girl with short red hair and glasses. "We're going to be best friends!" the girl told her. Ginger immediately doubted it. There was no way that Frances could be replaced.

To her dismay, the last two names to be called out for her form group were not unfamiliar to her. "Stephanie Sykes," called Mrs Masterson and Ginger's jaw hit the floor. Stephanie Sykes: the girl most likely to win *X-Factor* and be awarded the prize for services to the colour pink, giggling and flirting with boys. Her insides were just beginning to recover and the nausea pass when Mrs Masterson announced finally: "Milo Costigan".

There was no time to panic before she found herself being led cadet-style out of the hall and down a long corridor. Ginger's heart fluttered with the confusion of being mortified and delighted simultaneously as she walked behind Milo in his loose fitting trousers. Even his uniform looked cool!

Since the fateful toilet fiasco at Watford Gap services, Ginger had hardly thought of anything but Milo Costigan…

about how she had blown her chance to be cool... about how he knew her name and probably wouldn't forget it now... about how beautiful he had looked in his board-shorts and sun bleached hair...

She would have preferred to admire Milo from a distance, of say, fifteen classrooms and the canteen, but here he was in her form. This would mean he would also be sharing most of her classes and, inevitably, her every mistake and humiliation. Only girls PE would give her a break!

"Stand behind the chairs, class," directed Mrs Masterson before getting out a seating plan and studying the names carefully.

Despite her stress, Ginger was impressed by her new form tutor. Mrs Masterson stood out from the other tutors at the front of the hall. She was curvy with long shiny black hair and wore a look that suggested she could see into your soul from fifty paces. It almost made you feel afraid that she knew your secrets before she'd even spoken to you. Her dress sense was also pretty cool. She wore a tight black pencil skirt and red pussy-cat bow blouse and heels that couldn't be practical for work. This was a complete change from the pretty, casual, motherly primary school staff. Also, she sounded as though she were from Liverpool. Ginger decided that there was a good chance Mrs Masterson would be helpful in her own journey into adulthood. A role model at last! Mrs Masterson would recognise her as a kindred spirit and everything would be okay!

"Okay, guys. I'll call your name out and just follow my finger to your place. This seating plan will remain until the end of Year 7, unless I feel that there are extenuating circumstances that require you to be moved."

A small boy with tight curly black hair raised his hand: "Miss, what does extenuating mean?"

"It means, young man, that I will only adjust it in a case of life or death."

The class laughed respectfully, guessing this was Mrs Masterson being funny. A boy stood close to Ginger, nudged her and smiled. He looked friendly enough and she had to admit, he was rather well accessorised for a Year 7 boy. "I'm Tom," he whispered. "Who are you?"

"Erm, Ginge... Ginger. Ginger Mclean," she added, conscious of the dirty look the teacher was throwing at her. Perhaps she would be a tough nut to crack.

"Really? What a fabulous name!" he said at full volume, not seeming to care about school rules.

"Shush now! Right, Year 7, let me see..." Names were called out and children scrambled to their new places. With dwindling hope, Ginger felt sure that she would be placed next to Stephanie - a curse that she would be tormented by for the entire year to come. But then, when Stephanie was placed next to Tom, she knew there was only one possible final outcome: she would be seated next to Milo.

A sweat crept over Ginger's body as the reality of the situation was confirmed by the words from Mrs Masterson's carefully red lips. Her legs buckled slightly and again, she felt like she was going to be reacquainted with her Coco Pops.

Milo glanced over at her, as if he too was uncomfortable with the arrangement or, perhaps, because he couldn't work out Ginger's bizarre behaviour. He moved first. "Get a move on, erm, Ginger?" prompted the form tutor, impatient as the tall girl bumped her way across the classroom, ensuring eye contact wasn't made. Once seated, she kept her eyes firmly on a sign above the board which said 'PLANNERS OUT, PENS READY', her lips tightly fastened to avoid further humiliation.

Timetables were handed out, to be copied into fresh new planners. Though Ginger had been excited about the prospect of the planner, full of round spaces begging for House Points, she struggled to show enthusiasm. It was as if the story of the next nine months were written in the planner already: Monday 13th October – spelling test, PE kit and embarrassment; Wednesday 19th January: coaching session, food tech ingredients and humiliation.

The fact that Milo had almost the exact same timetable as her... the same groups... the same teachers... did not help matters. They had even got the same SATs scores! Then, eventually, Milo opened his mouth to speak: "Ginger, I meant to say..."

"What? What did you mean to say?" Ginger responded, surprised that when she finally spoke, she sounded full of aggression and suspicion.

"Oh, nothing. It doesn't matter," replied Milo, a hint of anger in his voice. Though she wasn't looking at him, she sensed his irritation at her response.

"What? Do you have something to say? Look, I'm sorry. I just feel kind of nervous today."

Ginger tried to relax and organised the contents of her pencil case into a neat colour order to help – nothing relaxed Ginger more than sorting out stationery apart from perhaps putting stuff into alphabetical order. She remained calm when his blazer sleeve brushed against hers.

"Well, I hope you don't mind me saying this but, erm, you've got something sticking out of your nose."

"What?" she blurted, confused, before realising what he meant. She quickly wiped her face, only to discover that a large greeny white blob was indeed now transferred to her finger. Her heart sank. Pain welled up behind her eyes. And yet, she simply smiled, packed her felt tips back into the *Coraline* pencil tin and, following the well-timed call to build dens, headed as quickly as possible for the door, followed closely by Tom, the boy with the nice accessories, shouting "Wait, Ginger, wait for me!"

"We HAVE to find Frances," Ginger mumbled into her hand and dragged Tom along with her like a spaniel.

The pupils were ushered outside to a playing field in their separate 'bands'. Ginger could just make out Frances and Rebecca in the distance, behind the ugly sports hall but she realised quickly that they wouldn't be catching up until later. She couldn't be sure but it looked like Frances was laughing. Ginger felt good that Frances was settling in and wished she could be more like her.

Bands were how teachers organised pupils, usually

according to what their SATs scores were but apparently also according to how noisy they were. Her band, 'R', was by far the quietest, though Stephanie could still be heard going on and on to some new followers about how amazing and popular she had been at primary school. Ginger gagged quietly and pretended to be interested in Mr Pearson's demonstration of how a den should be built.

The den that he revealed gave Ginger hope; in fact, it was the five star hotel of dens. "Yours can look nearly as good as mine!" he told the impressed looking pupils. It looked as though he had been working on the den since before the summer holidays and Ginger and Tom exchanged glances when they were given their bundles of den-making resources which did not include masking tape, canvas sheeting and a Sky Plus connection (like Mr Pearson's). Instead, they were given a girl called Brittany (who told them straight away that she believed in fairies and that fairies didn't like dens) plus some twigs, string and piece of camouflage netting.

Every other team had at least four in it, so Ginger's team was at a disadvantage. Also, given Ginger's long limbs, there was little chance she would be able to get into it, as per the rules. She tried to put her brain into 'prepare for failure mode', a strategy she had employed since Year 3. Whenever it looked unlikely that she would win, she would deliberately do the worst job she could. That way, she would know that she hadn't won because she hadn't tried rather than that she hadn't been good enough. Mostly, it worked a treat.

So Ginger, Brittany and Tom found a quiet spot of grass next to a tree where they could stand around looking as though they were discussing the best structure when in fact they were getting to know each other. Well, at least Tom and Ginger were. Brittany sat next to the tree and talked to her palm where her 'fairy' seemed to live.

The two bonded over a love for Jack Black movies... "ME TOO!" *Strictly Come Dancing...* "ME TOO!" and fizzy Vimto... "NO WAY! ME TOO!"

Stephanie Sykes and her team had taken the challenge somewhat more seriously. Somehow, Stephanie had also managed to get Milo on to her team. It was safe to say that she was bonding furiously. Ginger knew that Milo could be funny but from the laughter coming from Stephanie's mouth, it might has well have been Will Ferrell on their team. Where once there had been fluffy grass, there now stood a den that looked as though it might have been fitted with en-suite bathrooms.

Efficiently, Ginger assessed the situation. Den-building did not rank highly on Ginger's list of things that she wanted to be the best-in-the world-at. Had the team exercise been show-us-how-much-you-know-about-Greek mythology or create-a-sculpture-entirely-out-of-the-contents-of-your-pencil-case, then she would have used her time wisely. However, this new turn of events called for drastic action.

Ginger chewed on her lip.

It turned out that this was not a moment when she was prepared to fail.

Could she start out her new life at secondary school with this failure on her record? Did she really want to be known as the can't-make-a-den-for-toffee girl for the next twelve months?

"Right, Tom, we can't just stand around chatting about trivia. We have a den to build!" she demanded, pushing Tom out of the way.

"But I thought..." he managed, confused.

Like the Tasmanian Devil, Ginger went about dividing the meagre contents of their den-making kit. From her blazer pocket, she pulled out a very lovely Paperchase notebook and a pencil. In about twenty seconds she had drawn a diagram of something that looked like a den. Unfortunately, the den she had imagined would require a team of architects and at least four trips to Homebase.

She tore off the page and threw it at Tom, who caught it and gave it to Brittany who was now looking a little frightened of Ginger.

Another few minutes followed before Ginger said: "Right-oh, lose the fairies Brittany, we're building a den."

It took about ten more minutes for the structure to be in place. Only once did it collapse and that was because Brittany had climbed in to see if she could find the pixie that she had been talking to earlier.

Ginger and Tom took a moment to look at their creation, which by this time looked strong as it leant against the old ash tree. Secretly, they also surveyed the den on the next pitch, which Stephanie and her team had obviously decided was good enough to win because they were all sat around on the grassy verge and chatting.

"We can win this...." whispered Ginger in a way that worried Tom slightly.

To create further shelter, Ginger began gathering leaves and twigs that were hanging around in the late summer sun. She ordered Tom and Brittany to do the same and they followed her orders.

It only took a few minutes of them delving in the corners of the field for something to go wrong with the den.

A bell rang in a corner of the field to let the Year 7s know that they had just five minutes left and rushing back to their work, Ginger and her team found that where once the outline of a den had been, there was now just a pile of...

"What happened to our den...?" murmured Brittany. "Where will the pixies go...?"

Tom elbowed her in the ribs and said that if he ever heard her mention pixies again he would tie her to a tree using only her plaits and leave her there for the goblins to eat.

Brittany gulped.

"I d-d-don't understand..." stuttered Ginger. "What happened?"

"Over there," pointed Tom. "Our den got butchered by Miss Teen Pageant Barbie."

The group next to theirs had collected their things and were now speaking to Mr Pearson. The only member of the team left was Stephanie, who was lying on her side, apparently engrossed in a conversation with someone on her pink Blackberry phone.

Making eye contact with Ginger, she gave a little wink and rolled over.

The next few weeks of September were an avalanche of information, new routines and experiences. Ginger and Frances were hardly together except for at break and lunch times and for the journey to and fro. Having been in every class together for six years, this came as a shock for the friends. However, the rushed opportunities to deliver the details of their days were treasured.

Frances was enjoying school but was careful enough not to make too big a deal of this in front of Ginger who dramatically recounted every disaster with wild eyes and dangerous arm movements which made Frances roll around laughing. On the occasions when Ginger asked Frances how she was doing, Frances just shrugged and said it was better than she had expected.

After the nose incident and the den-building catastrophe, Ginger's days were spent putting all her efforts into keeping her nose clean (figuratively and literally) and completing her work to the best of her ability without drawing any further attention from the likes of Milo or that evil candyfloss head, Stephanie.

To his credit, Milo seemed happy to be ignored. However, his presence in virtually all her lessons gave Ginger a sense of constant terror. But even she had to admit, he was a worthy opponent when it came to matters of education. He could remember all his French verbs within a week. She found it harder to master but could quickly understand and use the new literacy skills they learned. She was throwing semi-colons and contrasting connectives around like they were old friends by the end of their first three weeks. Inevitably, she channelled her love into a sort of intense competitiveness and almost forgot how she had felt about him. It became an obsession by the end of the month; Ginger would literally go home and stomp around her bedroom when Milo had answered a question she couldn't or had got a sub-level above her in a subject.

She resolved that if nothing else went her way this year, she would at least be the best at school and if anyone noticed and liked what they saw, then, all the better.

It was Stephanie Sykes, however, who noticed the game that was being played between Milo and Ginger, in a rare moment when she wasn't thinking about: ...what goes with pink... more pink... are these shoes too high for an eleven-year-old... never...!

"Ginger, Ginger Mclean," she said, turning to face Ginger in a history lesson. Stephanie was smacking chewing gum between her tongue and the roof of her mouth - something that was strictly against school rules, thought Ginger.

"Do you love Milo Costigan?"

Ginger was knocked out by the question and decided to pretend she hadn't heard.

"You do, don't you? It is SOOO obvious. Me and Lydia were just saying. Are you trying to impress him with your geekiness?" She prodded Lydia to underline how clever and hilarious she was being to say this. "You know, he likes me. Of course. You need to get a life and a haircut. My advice to you is if you ever want a boyfriend, you need to quit being such a dweeb and put some make-up on. Who doesn't wear make-up? OMG, we're in high school!"

Ginger continued to pretend not to be listening to Stephanie until Milo eventually sat down next to her. Then she found herself being even frostier than usual: "Keep your planner on your side of the desk, would you? You take up too much room!" she told him, bitterly. Milo was used to her inexplicable mood swings and just did as he was told.

Stephanie turned around again, like some kind of defective wind-up doll: "Hi, Milo. I like your hair today." She purred again, and sort of winked at him, before responding quickly to their History teacher's command to face the front.

Ginger was horrified and too stunned by the disgusting act of flirtation she had witnessed with her own eyes to concentrate on the starter activity on the desk. Yet, Milo smiled to himself every now and then during the lesson and, whilst Ginger didn't really know why, she guessed he was drunk on love for Stephanie Sykes, just like the other boys.

At break time that day, Stephanie was in the refectory queue behind Ginger, Frances and Rebecca and insisted on talking really loudly about some made-up boy who liked her.

"I met him on holiday in Florida. He's called Brian but

his friends call him Buddy. He lives in Hollywood near Taylor Lautner and he's super rich. He was totally in love with me but I was like 'yah but I have to get home to my girls in England' and so he said 'well I'll come visit you, baby' and I was like…"

As she went on with her story her friends made little noises of approval like the tiny aliens in *Toy Story*.

Just as Ginger was sticking her fingers down her throat to show her disapproval, Tom from form turned up. He had been standing behind Stephanie and decided he would join Ginger and the girls in order to queue jump.

"Hi ladies, I'm queue jumping because…" Tom allowed his voice to increase in volume to a level which couldn't be ignored by Stephanie and her friends. "…I feel a bit ill after listening to Stephanie Sykes back there and her make-believe. If she's got an American boyfriend then I'm about to be announced as the new judge on *Strictly*. Actually, that is much more likely." He began to study the contents of the cold-food counter fridge. He picked out a cheese sandwich and finished, "Indeed, she's got all the intelligence and style of a Haribo Tangfastic."

Ginger, Frances and Rebecca laughed nervously as Tom flicked his fringe back and demanded a latte from the dinner lady as if he was in Starbucks.

Stephanie gave a 'huh!' and led her group out of the line amid complaints but clearly aware that Tom would be someone to steer clear of over the next five years at Atherton Academy.

When Ginger's Mum finally got round to asking how

things at school were going, Ginger answered with the usual 'fine'. It may not have been all she was expecting - no miracle had occurred and made her popular or cool; the mean girls were still mean. But she had survived and made a few new friends and, thankfully, kept disaster to a minimum. For now.

# October

*English Homework 14/10*
*POEM FOR AUTUMN by Ginger Mclean*

*Conkers! Oh poor conkers,*
*How I wish things for you were better,*
*If I knew your conker address,*
*I would send you an apologetic letter,*
*For all the beatings you endure,*
*At this violent time of year,*
*When you get smashed against your friend,*
*I wonder: do you shed a tear?*

It was a Friday night in mid-October. Satisfied with her 'Autumn Poem' for Mrs Masterson, who in addition to being her form tutor, also turned out to be her English teacher, Ginger scanned her homework timetable for the next assignment. *Nothing takes your mind off waiting for disaster like hard work*, she reflected, as she settled down to another science evaluation.

Reflecting on the last six weeks, she had barely raised her head from her books to look at the world around her. Frances was getting fed up with her for always being busy with work... too busy for hanging out and chatting, watching films, swimming and eating junk food. But the school work provided an excellent way for Ginger to escape the world and all its traumas.

"Why don't you come to my house? Let's play 'Princesses get chased by witch', just, you know, for old times' sake," suggested Frances on the walk home one day. Ginger kicked a pile of leaves and thought about it.

"Look, Frances, don't you think we are a bit old for that? I mean, we were too old for it in Year 2, really. We have BIG things to do now. I will never be a world famous United Nations leader if it gets out that in my spare time I like to play 'Princesses get chased by witch'."

Frances kicked a bigger pile of leaves and some of them stuck to her tights. She looked wounded, like a partly run-over hedgehog.

"Anyway, you need to work harder. Don't you have homework to do?" continued Ginger, trying to make Frances feel better.

"Erm, well yes. I suppose I do."

To try to make Frances feel better, Ginger began to hum „The Duck Song". Between them they thought that most of the hits on YouTube were down to them. Despite the gloom, Frances managed to join in and before long (and safely away from any other Atherton Academy pupils) they were in full swing of the song and singing at the top of their voices and nearly skipping through the leaf lined streets. They bumped into Adam just as they turned the corner into their avenue and sang even louder at him causing him to say 'losers' under his breath.

Closing the back door behind her, a sense of darkness enveloped Ginger. Home was a minefield at the moment, and with Adam always out with a new girlfriend and Alex back at Uni, only Ginger was there to see her parent's marriage falling apart at the seams. It was as if by doing her homework, she put on an invisibility coat. They would argue and bicker constantly about stupid domestic things like putting the bins out, but occasionally the rows seemed to have more significance. There had been something about a phone call. Mum was suspicious. Dad was defensive.

Recently, neither of them had paid much attention to her apart from to tell her how clever she was, heaping praise upon her when they remembered, but also placing pressure on her to perform. Everyone in the Mclean household expected nothing but the best from Ginger and sometimes, she felt it was the only thing anyone could see in her. But at least doing well in school was something she could control.

A text message bleeped from her phone: MEET AT

MINE TOMOZ 10AM TOM N REBECCA COMIN. C U THEN. XXX. It was from Frances.

Ginger pondered over it. She had to admit that some time with her friends was much overdue, otherwise she'd be sitting in the refectory alone for the rest of the year. And it was better than the usual Saturday morning horror of Mum trying to do the cleaning and getting on at Dad for not helping out. She decided to reply with: OK. C U THEN. TY. XXX

The homework couldn't be strung out any longer; she had completed the tasks set and the extension work and had started to use her highlighter pen imaginatively anywhere she could – a sure sign that it was time to pack up.

She looked around the bedroom, trying to refocus her eyes on anything that was more than 40 centimetres away. They were blurry from the two hours on close up work she'd been doing.

She had to admit, her room was pretty cool. Her and Mum had decorated it when they'd got back from France, guided closely by Alex's interior design advice. Between them, they'd created a sort of purple sanctuary. She'd had her favourite pictures framed, bought half of IKEA to house her clothes and books and tossed beautiful gold-trimmed cushions around. Her favourite old toys, the ones she couldn't bear to part with, were placed on a high shelf, reminding her of easier times. It was startlingly tidy and well organised, she noticed, as if looking at it through the eyes of an intruder. Just to make sure that the local burglars wouldn't be laughing at her from their dens, she ruffled the bed covers slightly and threw a couple of t-shirts on the floor. *Better*, she thought.

Her hamster, Trevor, had her own shelf. The cage was like an octopus, with play tubes shooting out of it to remind Trevor of her natural habitat in the wild. She had never seen any plastic tunnels on any of those BBC wildlife documentaries but the Pets at Home advisor had said to trust him.

Trevor ignored the tunnels and spent most of her time chilling out in a fluff ball or trying to create electricity in her wheel. Ginger rarely took Trevor out these days and she could be a bit moody and bitey.

Soon, she plugged her iPod speakers in, laid out on her bed and slept until morning when she was awoken by a clattering from downstairs and raised voices.

"Annabel, I'm miserable. Can't you see that? I'm nearly 50-years-old for God's sake and I need to start enjoying life. If you can't handle that then I'm going to her flat. She bloody appreciates me!"

"FINE, DAVE!" she could hear Mum scream, obviously through tears. "Just go! I want nothing more from you. You go to her and you never come back."

"Right then. I will," shouted her Dad - punctuating the argument with a door slam. The engine of his car started and then became faint, as it drove away.

Rolling over in bed again, Ginger thought that she could cry if she let herself, but if she did, she might not stop. She knew she ought to go and see how Mum was, but she didn't know what to say. Instead she pulled the duvet over her head until Mum came in and spoke to her. "Look, Ginger," she began, her face stained with rivers of tears from yesterday's make-up. "We need to talk about this. Your Dad, well…"

"Look, Mum, I heard," said Ginger, still submerged in lilac duvet and the flotsam of thick brown curly hair. "…and I don't want to talk about it."

"Nor do I but we have to, Ginger."

Her Mum sat on the edge of the bed and pulled her legs up to her chin like a child. It was too much for Ginger, she felt like the parent.

"Mum, just leave me alone," she said, too soon, before realising her words were selfish. Her Mum got to her feet unsteadily and left the room, closing the door behind her.

Immediately, Ginger felt terrible. She had no clue what to do about it so she turned her music on as loud as she could and set about getting ready for Frances'. She showered, attempted a blow dry which only succeed in giving her hair an electrified look, tied it back, applied Frizz Ease, applied some more, and then finally applied hair gel to the rebellious strands that continued to jut out.

Eventually, she also added a beanie hat.

She chose her clothes with as much precision as she would have her words in a story writing assignment in a literacy lesson. Skinny dark blue jeans, a long red shirt with small blue yachts printed on it, a blue scarf and some battered old blue Converse trainers. Neck down, she was happy with the result. Neck up, she looked about as happy as someone who had just witnessed the end of her parent's marriage. She resolved not to mention it to her friends that day - or perhaps ever, if she could help it.

As she organised her rucksack in the kitchen, her Mum came in and poured herself a glass of wine. A big part of her wanted to say "It's not even 10am, Mum!" but instead Ginger avoided her Mum's eyes and pulled away when she tried to touch her arm.

Why couldn't parents understand that it was hard enough being a child without having to witness the stupid lives of parents? Annabel and Dave were clearly idiots. And selfish ones. She would just have to look after herself.

The walk to Frances was refreshing, even though it was a matter of metres. Ginger felt like she'd got out of an oven and could breathe again. The autumn was turning colder and the wind was bitter, but it blew some clear space into Ginger's mind and it felt good.

She arrived at just the same moment as Tom, who had become a firm friend of the girls since he'd introduced them to some good tips for survival at high school.

Tom had come from a school from out of the area, a private school for rich boys whose parents hated them, he told them. He didn't know anyone at Atherton Academy, but he did know a thing or two about keeping the bullies at bay. This experience had come to him from years of being called 'gay', even in Junior School. "Where I was, if you weren't a rugby player with a broken nose, you were mincemeat. I only took a tube of concealer out one day after PE and the next thing you know, I was being hung up a peg by my tie. Outrageous!" he'd recalled.

The idea of a primary school boy even knowing that there was such a product as concealer delighted the girls and they immediately warmed to him. Especially because he had the guts to say and do the things they all wanted to.

And as for the comebacks! All those occasions when you wished you'd had an answer? They slipped from Tom like butter from a baked potato.

They went into Frances' house which was always tidy and smelled of fabric softener unlike Ginger's house which usually had the aroma of dog, despite Duke dying over six years ago. In her newly black bedroom, Frances was experimenting with clip-in hair extensions along with Rebecca.

"Becks is a genius with hair! Look what she's done to me!" Frances ordered and they had to admit, a miraculous makeover had taken place. Frances looked beautiful with her black hair straightened and fringe tucked behind her ear. She had also lost a lot of weight since July and it showed no sign of stopping. Ginger felt very proud of her best friend but at the same time wondered when *SHE* would begin to blossom into something less giraffe-like. Seeing this sense of wonderment, Rebecca offered to do her hair; who was Ginger to refuse?

"Here, grab a pen. We're going to rate the boys at school for cuteness," Becks instructed Ginger and Tom, who didn't seem to feel at all excluded - he seemed to have opinions on most things.

This was the kind of teenage activity Ginger had

secretly dreaded and as soon as the name 'Milo Costigan' came up, she thought she knew where the conversation was going. She picked up a pillow to hide behind in preparation and chewed down on the soft cotton.

Obviously, Frances had told everyone in the room about her crush on him and the horrific details of her many humiliations, so they had discussed him many times before. Ginger knew their opinions already. Milo got low marks from everyone apart from Tom who gave him 8 because he had nice hair. They did this to be kind to her, she was sure, as nobody could deny how beautiful Milo was.

Rumour had it he was going out with a Year 9 girl called Lucy Bagshott. Ginger didn't dwell on this. It didn't sound very likely. Lucy Bagshott was famously dim. Surely Milo had better taste?

They then moved on to a boy called Dermot Sandbach, who Becks claimed she'd heard fancied Frances. And then Archie Singleton, who Becks thought was the most attractive boy she'd ever seen. Better than Robert Pattinson? Better than Robert Pattinson.

Getting bored of this subject took hours, but eventually they settled down to some delicious treats made by Frances' Mum and to watch *Mean Girls* for the 67th time since Year 4.

It had taken a little while to get the thought of her Mum and Dad out of her mind, but by four o'clock, Ginger had forgotten all about it and was totally absorbed with the transformation to her hair Rebecca had been working on. It had taken about two hours to straighten and then curl into soft loops that framed her face, but the result was amazing. "OMG!" said Tom. "You look like Pixie Lott!"

Ginger took a few moments to look in the mirror and admire her reflection. In spite of herself, she found her lips forming a small pout.

On the way out, Frances stopped Ginger at the door. Though she looked like a goddess, Frances had that look on her face as if she had just been told that said 'but Father Christmas can't be a lie, he always leaves me a letter!'

"Is, erm, everything okay, Ginge? I mean with you, and erm, you know, your family?"

Something snapped in Ginger and she felt her body tighten.

"Everything is fine, Franny," she barked, not able to make eye contact. She focussed on fastening her shoe laces and turned her back to her friend.

"It's just that I saw..."

"You didn't see anything."

"Oh, right. Okay. See you on Monday. I'll text you?"

"Yep," murmured Ginger, her lips barely parting, her zip going up. She turned to leave and once again Frances stopped her.

"Your hair looks really nice, you know."

Ginger continued walking, knowing that the right thing to say would have been that Frances looked beautiful too, but somehow, the moment had slipped away.

When she left Frances' house, she was moving quickly. By the time she got to her front door, the presence of Dad's Renault was the last thing on her mind and she raced in to show off her new hair without a thought for the state she'd left her mother in.

Her parents were sat at opposite ends of the sofa, drinking cups of coffee like strangers. "Sit down, love," said Dad, fiddling with his glasses as he did when he was anxious. "We all need to talk."

"Love, we have something to discuss with you," went on Mum, who looked as though she hadn't brushed her hair that day. Ginger smoothed her own hair, as if just touching it could take her back ten minutes, to a time when it seemed important.

"The thing is, "interrupted her Dad, "…your Mum and I, we need some time a part. A separation…" he went on.

Ginger suddenly had an urge to call for Adam, but Mum told her they'd already spoken to him, when he briefly popped in to raid the fridge between a date and band practice. Frances' name came to mind but quickly she filed it away. She didn't feel ready to tell Frances. It seemed so important to keep her friends out of this. Above all, she wasn't ready to be known as one of the kids whose parents were breaking up. She wasn't one of them.

Feeling a cold draught from the window, she shivered. Her Mum would have said that 'someone was walking over her grave'. Had things been normal.

It was just her.

"I'm going to call Alex," Ginger eventually interjected, the pause becoming too much to bear.

She surprised even herself at how calmly she took the news. Her first reaction was that she wanted to talk to Alex, but not about the separation – she just needed to communicate with a family member who wasn't totally bonkers. Someone who made her feel secure and safe.

It was not as if the news was a great shock and to be honest, it had occurred to her before that divorce was a real possibility.

Lots of her friends' parents were divorced. Becks didn't even know her Dad. Tom just had his Mum.

But then there were families like Frances', where you could have mistaken them for those characters in TV adverts. Everyone was always hugging and laughing so much... there was hardly ever any swearing or door slamming. They went on holiday with other families to places like Spain and Greece and had barbeque parties and stuff. They got exactly what they wanted for Christmas and never seemed to forget things like PE kit or turn up at parents' evening. Ginger thought very angry thoughts as she pictured them sitting down to Sunday lunch and joking about other families that weren't as amazing as theirs.

It was just at that moment when Ginger's phone buzzed its buzzy buzz and alerted Ginger to a text.

She quickly reached for it, hoping that it would be from Alex but soon recognised Frances' name. Frances must have secret powers, she thought.

"GOT BAG OF M n Ms. WANNA STUFF YR FACE AND WATCH NICK TOMOZ? XOXO"

Ginger deleted it as fast as she read it and tried to make sense of the situation. She wasn't ready to confide in Frances. Frances couldn't possibly understand what she was going through. Though she had read enough young-reader novels and celebrity magazines to know that D-I-V-O-R-C-E was pretty common, it wasn't common enough in her neck of the woods. This would be the first problem that she hadn't trusted Frances with but then life had changed so much in the past few months, anyway. What difference was one more going to make? As a child of divorce she was bound to make some crazy decisions!

Back in her room, she was aware of a low level conversation in the hallway, followed by Dad shouting a goodbye and the door closing. Within seconds she found herself on the phone to Alex, who was shopping with friends. Ginger didn't mention what her parents had said. They just chatted about what Alex had been up to and the funny thing Tom had said to Mr Pearson on Wednesday. Alex always had time for her and it was a great comfort. Ginger guessed that Mum and Dad hadn't spoken to Alex yet, as she was sure that she would come home to see what was happening for herself.

Mum confirmed her suspicion when she came up to chat, half an hour later. "How are you, kitten?" she asked, sheepishly.

"Okay."

"Did you speak to Alex?"

"Yes."

Ginger became engrossed in an old issue of *Vogue* she had treasured for years.

"Did you tell her about... erm, you know?"

"We talked about school and clothes, Mum."

"You did? Well... that's good. We need to speak to her ourselves. Your Dad and I are going to drive over tomorrow and take her for lunch and a chat."

"Am I coming?" Ginger was suddenly interested, desperate to see her sister.

"No. Best not. I'll get Auntie Rachel to come over and keep you company."

"No need. I'm old enough to look after myself."

"Well, I suppose you are. You're doing better than me." Mum laughed in a way that Ginger didn't like. She looked down at her dreadful old tracksuit with the bleach stain on the zip and laughed again. "I look a mess. Who would want me?"

This was more than Ginger could manage; she was in no state of mind to deal with her mother's self-esteem issues. She had enough of her own.

Mum soon went off to have a bath and so Ginger tried to focus on her hair again. It looked great. She even felt that there was a possibility she wasn't that ugly and that one day, far away, a boy might notice her. Not a very gorgeous boy like Milo Costigan, but someone who had a glimmer of intelligence and, at least, some grasp of how often a teenager should take a shower.

The next day, Ginger woke up feeling a little dizzy. Her parents would get divorced, she realised. Dad seemed to have met someone else! He didn't live there anymore! The facts of the matter flooded her brain and she at once went to check her Mum hadn't done anything stupid, like dye her hair or get Botox. She hadn't. She was sitting doing paperwork at the dining room table, drinking herbal tea, waiting for Dad to pick her up. Ginger was shocked how little had changed and resolved to give herself an afternoon off homework - which was convenient as she had none left to do. Instead, as soon as Mum was out of the way, she would try to recreate the hair style Rebecca had introduced her to yesterday.

She started by washing it again and adding plenty of conditioner to make it shine. Then, she carefully blow dried it as straight as she could. Heating the GHDs Alex had passed on to her when she had her hair cut, she thought of seeing Milo the next day at school. He would be overwhelmed by her gorgeousness; he would melt and forget the nasty bogey incident; he would drop Lucy Bagshott in a flash!

The straightening went well and soon Ginger's hair was gleaming with health and shiny sleekness. Well, kind of. Not like it had yesterday, but close enough. But when she came to try the curls, the straighteners became tricky to wield. One curl went well, the next a matted mess. Just as she was attempting the fringe, they became tangled and wouldn't come out. She could smell the biscuity burning of her hair and began to panic. "Mum! Mum," she shouted, forgetting that Mum was sixty miles away with Dad and Alex.

Eventually, she dislodged the straighteners and looked in the mirror to find that her hair resembled Mike's girlfriend's in Monster's Inc. The flood-gates opened and she began to cry big fat tears that puddled on the laminate floor.

Ginger felt useless and ugly and that, in some way, her parents would not have split up if she hadn't been born. She crawled up into the foetal position, trying desperately to wish the world away…

She was disturbed from her unscheduled slumber when the phone began to ring. It was Alex.

"How are you, Ginger?" asked Alex, carefully. She must have been able to hear that her younger sister was obviously crying. Ginger couldn't answer, the tears just came heavier and she struggled to breathe through them. Big gasps were all that Alex could hear down the phone line.

"Look, Ginger. I've seen Mum and Dad. They've set off home. It'll be okay, you know? Don't cry, you'll make me." And she did. Both girls cried down the phone to each other for five minutes, neither speaking a word of sense. But it felt good to have her sister close, thought Ginger, and be able to let her feelings out. If nothing else went right, she would always have the best sister anyone had ever had.

However, Alex wasn't there when the next catastrophe struck. It was Adam that found her sitting on a bench across the road from their house the next day after the worst ever day of school.

Ginger was wondering how the gods and goddesses could be so cruel and taking big gulps of increasingly cold air. The weather was changing.

In her hand she held a crude drawing on a crumpled

piece of paper. The paper, she noticed, was of a poor quality and the felt tips had blurred slightly as big salty tears dropped on to it. Yet, she couldn't stop staring at it.

The drawing was of a girl with legs like a daddy long legs, arms as long as an orang-utans, google eyes and hair that looked like a microphone. There were labels on the drawing pointing at different parts of the girl. They said things like 'hair is made of cheese-straws' and 'lips that can be used to stick to a car windscreen'. Her least favourite though was the label pointing at her legs: 'too skinny and hairy.'

Ginger hadn't given any thought to her legs. She had always thought that they were at worst 'okay', if a little thin and pale.

Moreover, they were so far away from her eyes that she hadn't noticed that they were hairy, not hairy or anything in-between. Did she have time to shave them? Wasn't that for grown-ups who had nothing better to do? Did she really want to take a pink-handled blade to them? It seemed like she would probably have to or invest in thick tights that made her itch.

Another huge deluge of tears fell from her face.

Suddenly, something moved in front of the sun and she looked up to see Adam.

As usual he had huge ear-phones stuck to his head and a sweater that looked as though it was made for someone four times bigger than him. It hung to his knees and made him look even lankier than he was.

He didn't make eye contact but played with his phone as

he asked her, reluctantly, if she was alright.

Ginger couldn't speak but managed to hold up the drawing.

Instantly, Adam understood the problem.

"Come with me," he told her, awkwardly.

Ginger followed him to the house. Mum wasn't home from work yet so they were safe to do whatever he planned. Ginger hoped it wasn't to remove the hair from her legs as that was NOT something that she wanted to share with Adam.

Inside, Adam placed the drawing on the counter-top. Then he took out some scissors from the drawer. These were the special scissors that Mum used for cooking. If she had caught them being used for anything else she would have had a fit.

Adam cut the drawing up carefully, until it was in tiny strips that fluttered onto the floor.

He then gathered them up and told her to follow him again. He led her into her bedroom, which made Ginger even more nervous. Adam was not allowed in there unless it was to tell her to get out of the house in the event of a nuclear attack.

Then, he opened Trevor's cage. In the corner, where Trevor did her stinky business, he placed the bits of paper and squashed them down so they absorbed the yuckiness. He then took his arm out and fastened the cage. Finally, he took a seat on the edge of the bed and took out his phone to study.

Ginger wondered how long he would stay there. Yes,

she liked his plan so far but she didn't want to have him there all night.

Two minutes later, at most, Trevor woke from her peaceful slumber and did one of her giant yawns. A moment later, she lumbered over to her hamster toilet and did her business. Ginger could just make out the word 'hairy' before it dissolved under the hamster wee.

"There we go. Good work, Trev," drawled Adam. "Doesn't that feel better?" he said to Ginger, making eye contact for one glorious moment before stomping out.

And what do you know, it did. A little bit.

# November

AUDITIONS NIGHT FOR

*ATHERTON ACADEMY YOUTH ORCHESTRA*
TUESDAY 4TH NOVEMBER
PERIOD 6
*BRING YOUR INSTRUMENTS AND*
*PERMISSION FROM PARENTS/CARERS IN*
*PLANNER*

"So, Miss Ginger Mclean, will you be wowing the judges with your cello-tastic skills?" asked Tom after Mrs Masterson read out the notice in form time one Monday morning. Somehow, Tom had managed to sweet talk their teacher into moving seats to a position which was directly behind Ginger, allowing him to communicate with her more easily. Since she had found the drawing in her English book, she had felt pretty lonely in lessons. It was becoming harder to get out of bed and go to school every day. She prayed that nobody had seen the stupid thing. Nobody, of course, except the culprit.

She was impressed by Tom's powers of persuasion as she herself had tried on various occasions with excuses ranging from 'the radiator antagonises my (non-existent) eczema' to 'wouldn't it be better if I were placed next to someone I could be a role model to – Milo Costigan doesn't need any help'. However, Mrs Masterson was a tough cookie to break and had just given Ginger a smile which read as 'not on your life'.

"Hmmm. I dunno…" replied Ginger, certain that Tom's question would grab the interest of Milo. Ginger knew from primary school music lessons that Milo was a brilliant clarinet player. He had often played in school assemblies and it was widely known that he went to some big orchestral group in Manchester at weekends.

"You totally should," added Tom before being asked *again* by Miss whether or not he'd had his planner signed by his Mum.

"No. She was busy last night having another face lift,

Miss."

"Really, Tom? Is that true?"

"Yes! Of course it is. It's her third. Her face is starting to look like a dog's bum, Miss."

Mrs Masterson chuckled throatily and moved on to Ginger and Milo's table. "Fancy trying out for the orchestra, you two?" she asked them. "Sounds like a great opportunity. The orchestra is really good. They take part in lots of competitions. Best of all, they always play at school events. It will really build your confidence up; you never know, it might help you to get to know each other, too."

Her work done, Mrs Masterson went over to talk to Stephanie about how short her skirt was.

Ginger and Milo both blushed and as the bell rang, they practically jumped out of their seats to increase the distance between them. This resulted in them bumping into each other with as much force as they had put into avoiding each other. Everyone laughed.

Ignoring them, Ginger remembered that Performing Arts was next and that it was a rare chance to catch up with Frances and Rebecca, who shared their set. Her real friends!

Unfortunately for Ginger, the class today was going to be in dance as their drama teacher, Miss Grey, was away on a course. Two groups of thirty were squeezed into the dance studio along with one very grumpy teacher.

The dance studio was a nightmare for many of the pupils of Atherton Academy: mirrors everywhere, the odour of sweaty jazz shoes, a lack of fresh air which made them claustrophobic and a dance teacher, Mr Armstrong, who reminded Ginger of Craig Revel Horwood from *Strictly Come Dancing*. He was mean.

"You're all elephants today!" he screamed as he instructed the uncoordinated Year 7s to stretch and move around the room as though they were Broadway performers. Much bumping and 'sorries' were heard around the room. Two boys clashed and a fight even broke out, before Mr Armstrong finally instructed them to find a space on the floor to sit.

Ginger sat as close to her friends as possible and concentrated on avoiding eye contact with Mr Armstrong who had a bad habit of picking on you to demonstrate a complicated street-dance manoeuvre in front of the class. He had a special sense for choosing the least talented dancers in the group which was often funny unless, of course, that person was you. Still, even Ginger had to admit, it was better than him choosing one of Stephanie Sykes crew, who, sensing such a moment coming on, would pound the air with their fists and squeal "Sir! Sir!" to be picked. Watching Stephanie in her sparkly dance shoes, leg warmers and leotard was too much.

Mercifully, Mr Armstrong chose a boy who could actually dance today and so a tsunami of relief swept across the Year 7s and everyone began to relax a bit. The pumping music was dreadful, yes, but Year 7s moved around without self-consciousness. However, Frances began to look a bit pale and so Ginger asked Sir if she could take her friend to the toilet.

Frances headed for a cubicle as Ginger began to read the new graffiti on the wall. It was painted over pretty quickly usually so you always knew the writing was fresh. Just as Frances began to say something from beyond the swing door, Ginger was horrified to see a name that was not unfamiliar to her...

"GINGER MCLEEN HEARTS MILLO COSTIGAN. T.L.N.D!"

"Urrggh, what? What did you say Ginger...?" came Frances voice.

"It SAYS... Ginger Mclean hearts Milo Costigan, on HERE! Oh my God!"

"But Ginger, what are you talking about... Look, I need your help...my, urm, period has started I think!" But Ginger had long forgotten about her best friend in the toilet. She was too busy searching for a Tippex tube in her bag... a marker pen... anything to clean the wall of the work of the evil culprit who couldn't spell.

"They've not even spelt it right!" she screamed, firstly trying to correct the spelling before checking her behaviour and rubbing at the marker-pen lettering until her fingers were close to bleeding. It must have been written in Sharpie!

"But, Ginger, did you hear me? My period has started and I don't know what to do..."

"This is outrageous!" screamed Ginger.

"Just get me something from the machine, will you? Or go tell the school nurse. Just do something, Ginger! Ginger? GINGER!" Frances shouted.

"What? Erm, yes, right. Just a minute. I have something in my bag." Ginger managed to get back to class to retrieve a Tampax she had in her bag. Being tall, she supposed, had meant that she had started her periods at the end of Year 6. It seemed so stupid to make a big deal of it, she thought. The matter of the graffiti was much more pressing.

Back in the toilet, after some garbled excuse to Mr Armstrong about women's problems, Ginger passed the tampon under the cubicle door to Frances, who seemed to be quite upset.

"I know!" Ginger said, assuming that Frances was also upset by the graffiti. "What a totally idiotic thing to do. It's off now – we'll never mention it again."

"Ginger, why is it always about you?" came Frances' reply. "This is my first period and don't even know what to do with a tampon. In a minute I'm going to come out there and stick it up your stupid long nose!"

Harsh, thought Ginger, as she began to describe how a Tampax worked.

Fifteen minutes later, the two girls made it back to dance class. Frances looked a little uncomfortable, but more angry than anything. She went to sit between Rebecca and Stephanie, avoiding the spot on the studio floor where there was a space next to Ginger.

Ginger didn't understand what she'd meant. Surely she'd always been around for her friend? They'd shared everything since Year 1! Why couldn't Frances see how terrible it was to read misspelled graffiti about yourself on a toilet wall? And the nose comment!

After school that day, the two girls walked home lost in their own thoughts. When it began to rain, Frances pulled the hood up on her parka. Ginger had no hood and felt the drizzle spritzing her hair with its magic frizz potion. A leaf blew off a tree and stuck to her cheek and her thin wool gloves absorbed the icy wetness, making her fingers tingle. The day was not a good one.

She considered who the graffiti culprit could be. It didn't take an astrophysicist to work out that it was Stephanie Sykes or one of her cronies. The only thing missing were love hearts to dot the 'i's'. But even Ginger couldn't explain why Stephanie had bothered to do it. Stephanie had nothing to gain from such mindless bullying. Her very existence on the same planet was enough punishment for Ginger. Seeing her get changed in PE wearing a pink push-up bra decorated with plastic crystals and smothered in orange fake tan was enough to bring on Ginger's gag reflex.

There had to be more to it. Ginger must have really annoyed Stephanie and she wracked her brain for an explanation. The scary thing was, if something was annoying Stephanie, there was a chance that she would use more than a black Berol marker pen as a weapon. The possibilities were terrifying.

After school, Ginger arrived at the bridge next to the playing field where she always met Frances for the walk home. She felt full of emotion and was keen to make amends with Franny so that they could talk about it. When Frances arrived Ginger began to launch into a discussion about the day.

"I'm sorry that you got your period... erm, well, no, actually it's great that you got your period! Welcome to the club! Anyway, who do YOU think wrote that rubbish in the toilets? It HAS to be Steph..."

It took them to get to the end of Cyprus Avenue before Ginger noticed that Frances hadn't said a word back to her. Not a single theory! Nothing! When they arrived outside Ginger's house, Frances just crossed the road. Ginger called out "See ya later, alligator" but all she got in reply was "Yeah, later".

Ginger decided not to dwell on it; this was no time for friendship issues.

At home, her Mum was busy with bundles of paperwork. She went over to say hello and offer to make her a cup of tea before she headed up to her room to begin her own bundle of homework.

She could hear Mum moving around downstairs and then the Poirot music come on the television.

Mum loved detective books and TV shows. She always bragged that she knew at least two-hundred ways to commit a murder or steal jewels without being caught. She'd shout things like 'Ha! School boy error, young fellow!' at the screen as she watched.

Ginger worried that Mum would grow to hate Dad so much that he would be found face down in a flower bed one day with no sign of an explanation.

The past few weeks had been tense between mother and daughter. Ginger naturally took her Mum's side in most things but, somehow, the break-up had put an ocean between them. Mum had been busy with sorting out all the practicalities of becoming a single parent since Dad had moved out. There had been little opportunity for quality time. She wondered if her Mum had noticed. Ginger also suspected that she was making things worse. Sometimes, Ginger knew she was just being a pain for the sake of it. For example, she moaned when Mum asked her to empty the dishwasher, made a big deal about what was for tea and criticised her Mum for everything. Was she deliberately trying to hurt her Mum, she asked herself? She didn't like the answer to that question – she was sure that she was. But then, Mum seemed so numb to what was going on. Like she didn't care that the atmosphere in the family home was like a very messy funeral parlour.

"Hey, Mum. What are you up to?" Ginger enquired, trying to sound breezy and positive.

"Well, it's just all this money stuff, love. It's complicated."

"Can I make you a cup of tea?" asked Ginger politely, like she wasn't talking to the person who had given her life, but another adult – a family friend or an insurance salesman.

"Um, yes. That would be nice," replied Mum, finally looking up at her daughter with an expression that said 'who has taken Ginger away and replaced her with a kind and helpful human being'. But the look was fleeting and quickly Mum started to shuffle documents around again and make grumbling noises to herself.

Ginger made the tea – Lapsang Souchong – her Mum's

favourite, and then retreated up the stairs with a heavy heart.

Since Dad had left, she only saw him once a week. She had had to reorganise her homework timetable in order to give over her Sundays to doing lame stuff with him. Usually this involved visiting somewhere educational like a museum or gallery and then a silent, awkward meal at Pizza Express. Sometimes, Dad would try to get into her good books with a stationery gift or an iTunes voucher. Sometimes he would enquire about school and her friends. Often, he would just look at her in a way that seemed so sad and hopeless that Ginger would have to concentrate on a dough ball.

Once in her room, Ginger's eyes were drawn to the cello that was leaning against the book case. She hadn't practised much recently, with everything that was going on. Her teacher, Miss Peasgood, had told her that she was developing lazy habits and that if she wanted to be entered for Grade 4, she'd need to pull herself together.

Looking at the clock, Ginger decided she could give up half an hour to some cello practice. Tonight's homework was limited to a few easy algebra questions and reading a chapter of the book they were studying in English. Perhaps she'd give the orchestra auditions a go… what did she have to lose?

Peeling open the cello case, the familiar smell of resin and dust brought back memories of primary school. She and Milo had passed each other on their way to see the peripatetic music teachers every Wednesday, hardly acknowledging one another. How things hadn't changed!

At first, her cold fingers wouldn't do as they were told and the sounds that came out of the instrument were about as musical as a frightened cat. She practised her scales a few times to warm them up and eventually retrieved a sheet of music that she knew she could play. Moments later, Ginger Mclean was lost in the music.

It felt good to play and Ginger felt a little better about everything within half an hour. Tomorrow she would try-out for the orchestra and if that meant spending more time with Milo Costigan, then so be it. At least she wouldn't have to deal with Stephanie who had been far too bothered about becoming a Prima Ballerina in Year 4 to take up an instrument. Though she carefully placed the instrument back in the case, Ginger slammed it shut, imagining Stephanie's fingers were carelessly positioned at the join.

The school theatre was a 'modern masterpiece of light and inspiration', or so the school prospectus had read at Open Evening a year earlier. Everyone called it the 'Atrium' though Ginger guessed that only about twelve people knew what that meant. She had looked the word up in the small school dictionary she carried in her bag for such occasions as this and felt mildly superior about her discovery.

None of this was of much comfort now, however, as nervous young musicians sat around in clusters. Some of the more serious of the hopefuls were sitting alone as they tuned their instruments and got into their 'zones'.

Ginger sat high up on the amphitheatre seats, looking

down at the stage and, out of the corner of her eye, at Milo Costigan and his skater friends who all played some instrument or another. Most played rock air-guitar as they waited, an instrument Ginger had never seen in a formal orchestra.

Milo was twirling his clarinet like a majorette and chatting to a boy with bushy brown hair and an earring – a boy from Year 10, she guessed. It never ceased to amaze her how people were drawn to him – how easy it was for him to mix with older kids. It was different for boys.

Ginger wished Frances was there to share the experience. She looked down at her hand to where Frances' should have been and thought about the follow-up conversation they'd had the night before.

Frances had been wheeling out the wheelie bin, which was her chore every week. In exchange for this one job she received a ton of pocket money that she generally spent on postcards of Labradors and sponsoring puppies at the Dogs' Trust. Recently, she had noticed that Frances had begun to spend her cash on things like make-up and hair products; she had even heard Frances talk about using it to download the most 'amazeballs' songs that she had everyone was talking about at school. Ginger had been in the front garden searching for a wintery object to draw for her art homework and had sheepishly gone over to say hi and ask if Frances was going to the auditions to try out with her violin. Ginger had never told her but she thought she was really good.

"No, I don't think so," said Frances, finding a tree over

Ginger's shoulder particularly interesting as she rubbed her hands together to warm them.

"Oh, that's a shame. We could have talked about what an idiot Stephanie Sykes is whilst we waited. You could bring some M and Ms."

"Well, I'm really busy with other stuff. I hope it goes okay for you though," said Frances and then, she was gone.

Ginger put it down to Frances' period starting. Some people got weird about that.

The quality of the performances varied. There were around thirty auditionees, mostly from Year 8 and 9. Some hadn't made it last year, but the word was that Mr Arnold, the music teacher, had been told to take everyone who showed an interest. That meant that there was little chance of failure today and although Ginger was by nature competitive, she felt unusually relaxed.

Milo went up on the stage first. Mr Arnold told him to take his time, enjoy the setting and give them his best shot.

The result was beautiful. Milo played some jazz tune, the kind of thing that you might hear in an expensive restaurant. The sound was mellow and summery on the cold, wet November evening and everyone stopped to listen. Even Mrs Montgomery, the head teacher, popped her head though the Atrium doors and joined in with the grand applause when he finally allowed his cheeks to release the last mouthful of air.

Ginger was transfixed. She had known Milo could play but the loveliness of his music was unexpected. Part of her wanted to cry. She remembered briefly why she had always liked Milo. He was different and special. Perhaps he was like her. Perhaps he felt the same pressures? Perhaps not: why would Milo ever need to worry about human stuff – he was undoubtedly some kind of angel pretending to be a Year 7 boy.

Quickly she put these thoughts out of her mind – they were not helpful – and was called to the stage. Ginger half hoped that Milo wouldn't stay for the rest of the audition but to her dismay, he re-joined his friends with a series of high fives and sat down respectfully to listen to her performance.

For a second, he seemed to lean into the palms of his hands, as if he was preparing to concentrate on Ginger like she was of some interest to him. Probably, he was waiting for her to mess things up.

As it happened, though her fingers were shaking like skeletal leaves on an autumn tree, Ginger made the cello work for her. She played Dvorak's 'Humoresque' and though it was basic by Milo's standards, it didn't sound half-bad. Mr Arnold clapped enthusiastically as he helped her pack the instrument away and asked her what grade she was. "You'll be a great asset to the orchestra, young lady. Welcome aboard!"

"Thanks, sir," managed Ginger, focussing on keeping the moment of victory going long enough for her to get down the stage steps.

Passing Milo was unavoidable, she noticed, as her bag and coat were still high up in the Atrium. Carefully looking at her shoes, she nearly tripped when she heard Milo call out to her.

"Hey, Ginger."

"Ah, err, hi Milo."

"You're good," he said standing up to face her awkwardly.

"Thanks, um, so are you. But you're really good, you know," Ginger managed, thinking that this conversation wasn't going too badly.

"I like the cello. I am rubbish with strings. I'm impressed."

"Well, it's easy. I'm sure you could play anything you wanted to, if you tried," said Ginger, shyly.

The butterflies in her stomach seemed like they were sure to rush out if she let the conversation continue so she said a nervous "Seeya" and headed up the steps, slipping only once on the ascent.

Ginger emerged from the audition with a smile that stretched from ear to ear. But then looking out of the tall reception windows into the dark, wet November evening, her heart sank at the thought of the walk home. She decided to give her Mum a call to see if she could pick her up. Mum answered on the second ring and agreed.

Fifteen minutes later she was squeezing her cello into the car's boot. Mum looked to be in a good mood.

"Darling, I do sometimes wish you'd chosen to play the violin. Something small," she laughed. "We could downsize from this great whale of a car and get something small and sporty."

Satisfied that the huge case wasn't blocking her rear

view mirror, she set off down the drive.

"How about we treat ourselves? What do you say to hitting the shops and eating at Nandos?"

"Mum, I think that's the best idea ever," replied Ginger as Mum took a left at the lights towards the shopping centre on the other side of town.

Later that month, Ginger was feeling a little more settled at home and things had fallen into some kind of routine. She still toyed with the idea of creating a *Parent Trap* but fell short of an identical twin to conspire with. Ginger wondered whether, if she did have an identical twin, she would be the evil pretty one or the not-so-pretty one with brilliant maths skills. It didn't take her long to decide which one she was and which one she would rather be.

If she could just bring herself to sort out the weirdness with Frances, they could make a plan just like the ones they had made when they were little.

That week there was a special cooking workshop being held during period 4 and 5 on Tuesday. A real chef had come in to teach them to be brilliant master-chefs. Pupils had been selected in that weird way the pupils are selected for things like that. Teachers prepared for lessons much like Capital people in the *Hunger Games*. A flipping raffle. Mostly, as she looked around, the thing that all of them had in common was a neat tie and a good behaviour record. Teachers were really careful about which pupils they put in front of outsider-civilians. They were fussy about things like whether the Year 9 had tattoos or was having a baby...

This would have been the perfect opportunity to make a plan with Frances, who also turned up at the technology classroom with Rebecca and some of her class. But something got in the way and despite her best efforts, she couldn't even make eye-contact with Frances.

Then, the moment was passed and she found herself paired-up with Tom.

As they tried to replicate the recipe, the pair discussed the general horribleness of being a nearly-teenager whilst also doing occasional impressions of the pretentious and angry chef.

Then Tom said something that made her think.

"You know, it must be great to be beautiful and stupid. But I still think that you'd have problems. You think that if you were less gangly or less good at using speech marks, your life would be better. But it is just the same for everyone. I worry just like you. Yes, I have great eye-lashes and yes, I have a bitingly clever wit, but I'm still human. I still cry sometimes when I think that I have to do a cross-country run with the rest of the animals in this year group."

Tom studied the contents of a tub of mixed herbs for a moment, sniffed it, pulled a face and then poured most of it into the pasta sauce that was bubbling in a saucepan.

Rebecca came over and asked Ginger formally if she and Frances could borrow some of their olive oil. Ginger handed it over and tried to make conversation but Rebecca had already gone.

She turned back to Tom and he shrugged.

"I think what I'm trying to say is that it is rubbish being a kid and probably just as hard being an adult. I mean, what the heck is a tax return? I have no idea but it seems to be on my Mum's mind a lot,"

"But you are always so cool," said Ginger, at the same time, tasting a mouthful of pasta to see if it was cooked. "I just wish I could be cool about it all, like you."

"Yeah, you think I'm cool. Do you think anyone else thinks so? I just seem cool because I hang around with losers like you!"

Ginger slapped him across the face with a tea-towel and they both laughed.

"Just remember that you aren't the only one who is miserable sometimes."

"That doesn't actually make me feel any better at all."

"Sometimes, Ginger," Tom crinkled his eyes and put on an American accent, "your pasta is just the right side of cheesy. Other times, it'll taste like arm-pit."

"Deep, Tom. That is so deep."

"Yeah well, good times and bad times aside, you do have friends and we like you quite a lot."

Ginger blushed.

"That's lovely of you say Tom, but, you know, sometimes I just wish I could be a better friend to everyone else. Especially Frances."

Ginger glanced behind her to where Rebecca and Frances were working. Frances had just poured the pasta straight into the sink instead of the bowl.

That was her Frances.

# December

*Dear Father Christmas,*

*Although I haven't thought for a moment that your existence is anything more than a trick to fool small children into behaving themselves since I was six, I would like to offer you some suggestions for gifts that you may or may not bring me. Obviously, I am addressing you, Mum, here. Anyway, take note:*

*1 pair of Chanel ballet shoes (pg. 27, Grazia) Size 7*

*1 Alexander McQueen skull scarf (Net-A-Porter)*

*2 or more Chocolate Oranges*

*1 ring-binder folder*

*2x Sanctuary bubble bath*

*3 x John Frieda Frizz-Ease Christmas Gift Set*

*1 large pencil case*

*1 Cath Kidston school-appropriate sized bag*

*30x pairs of socks*

*£40 iTunes vouchers*

*World peace*

*Yours sincerely,*

*Ginger Mclean.*

Christmas was Ginger's favourite time of year and despite the weirdness of Dad not being around, Ginger felt the familiar sparkle of the season in every part of her body.

She tried hard to fight it. Of course, there was much about Christmas that Ginger disapproved of. To begin with, novelty earrings were beginning to blossom from ears. It was perfectly acceptable for Mrs Azzaro in the newsagents to wear tiny festive parcels from her lobes, but the sight of them on her school mates was truly depressing. Dangling chubby Santas and fairy-lit trees would be everywhere in registration; fortunately, for everyone who had taste, Mrs Masterson saw to it that these were removed before you could say 'We three kings'. Ginger hoped that along with adhering to rules schools, Mrs Masterson was exhibiting excellent taste in these matters – steering her form away from fashion disaster. Needless to say, Stephanie Sykes was the proud owner of at least twenty-seven pairs of spangled Christmas crimes.

Another irritation for Ginger was the Christmas light competition that had sprung up on her street. Frances' family were the worst for this display of grotesque Christmas spirit. This year she'd heard her claim that her Dad had spent £400 on the illuminations. Not only was Santa hanging on for dear life from the chimney, but 'Seasons Greetings' magically flashed 24/7 in the dim December light. According to Tom, Frances was worried that there would be no money left for the new iPhone she'd been hinting about.

Frances' news only got to Ginger these days via Tom or

overheard conversations. Ginger had started walking to school on her own most days because Frances often got a lift with her Mum. It was starting to be obvious that she was being avoided.

Ginger was waiting in the usual spot on the first Monday of the month, ready to walk home and chat about all the things they always talked about at that time of year like what they wanted for Christmas and who would be first member of their families to meltdown on the big day. But as it got darker, Ginger realised that Frances wasn't coming.

Getting out her phone after about fifteen minutes, she hurriedly texted her friend with what she hoped was a tone of bright and breeziness.

HANDS GONE NUMB! WHERE ARE YOU? XXXX

But there was no reply.

REALLY COLD! THINK I JUST SAW A REINDEER WEARING THERMAL LEGGINGS. WHERE ARE YOU? XXXX

Again, there was nothing.

It was only 4 p.m. but it began to feel like the witching hour. Only die-hard rugby players were coming out of school now, looking ruddy faced from an after school blood-bath fixture. They entirely ignored the tall Year 7 girl with the gigantic instrument and look of misery on her cold face.

She gave up and began to struggle down the path towards the sports fields, thinking back to all the great memories they had shared at Christmas together.

There had even been one year when the Mcleans had gone over for Christmas Eve drinks with the other neighbours. Dad had been quite tipsy and insulted Frances' Dad about his conifers.

The annual shopping present buying trip they had shared since Year 5 wouldn't happen this year. She could go with Tom and it would be great but Tom wouldn't like the same shops. She was so grateful to him for being her friend and loved him a lot, but nothing could replace the increasing hole in her heart where Frances should have been.

It was nine o'clock one Sunday in mid-December when Mum asked her if she wanted to bake some biscuits to decorate the tree with – a tradition that had been honoured since Ginger was old enough to wield a cookie cutter.

"It might even cheer you up!" said Mum.

Even though Ginger didn't like to show too much enthusiasm for anything these days – she feared that it was a bit primary school to get giddy – she joined her Mum in the kitchen with freshly antibacterialised hands.

Mum had also been working hard to ensure that the kitchen was free from dangerous toxins and clutter – a task that had taken her since 6am, Ginger guessed. She'd lit a cinnamon and berry candle and put a classical radio station on to further set the mood.

Recently, Mum had seemed really positive. Christmas was occupying her thoughts and left little time to worry. Even her work seemed to be going well – something that was rare for social workers, Ginger guessed. Her Mum's job often involved working with families where there was no money and, often, not much love. Mum wasn't hardened to it. She would sometimes cry in the bath after a tough day and then drink an extra glass of wine or two.

"Get the ingredients out, would you, Ginger," instructed Mum cheerfully as she climbed on a stool to reach into the dusty baking cupboard above the fridge. "Stars, reindeers or Santas?"

"Hmm," considered Ginger, arranging the butter, flour and sugar in a neat TV chef-ish sort of line on the counter. "I think just stars would be nice."

"Yes, I agree," replied Mum grabbing the cutter box and jumping down to the floor.

They worked in silence, Ginger disposing of the stars that Mum cut out that weren't quite symmetrical. Mum did not have very high standards when it came to that kind thing. She said that she was happy for the decorations to look rustic. Ginger had heard her use the word 'rustic' to describe anything that she made that looked like a seven-year-old had crafted it in Golden-Time.

Just as the stars were going into the oven, Adam appeared at the door with his hair fluffed up – a sure sign that he was meeting his new girlfriend, Agnes.

"Right-oh, I'll see you later," he said, checking his coat for his phone and wallet. "Err, Mum…"

"I gave you twenty quid yesterday! Surely…"

"But I promised I'd get her a Christmas present today, Mum." Alex did his best down-hearted look – all big eyes and sunken shoulders. Mum was a sucker for this. Alex could ask for the world and get the universe. Or more likely, fifty quid when he asked for forty.

He stuffed the cash into his pocket and kissed Mum on the cheek before skipping out the door in a very unmanly fashion for a six foot, seventeen-year-old.

Mum rolled her eyes and smoothed down her pretty tea dress. Pretty tea dress? Ginger suddenly noticed that Mum was also wearing some make-up. On a Sunday morning in December? "Mum, um, you look really nice today. I like your hair like that, too." Mum looked pleased with herself and smiled coyly.

Mother and daughter then got on with the cleaning up, enjoying the time together but each sensing that the other probably had something to say.

Nobody said anything that might have ruined the lovely atmosphere. They were the picture of mother and daughterly peace and understanding.

Alex was expected to be home from university later that afternoon and they talked about what they should all do that night. They guessed what kind of stories she would have for them. Mum worried that none of the stories would involve late nights cramming in the library. Adam had promised to be home for dinner so all three of them could get together. Dad was taking Ginger out for lunch at half eleven.

Though Ginger had argued that it wasn't fair that Adam got out of the Sunday ritual of going out with Dad, it hadn't done much good. Adam met him for a game of squash on Friday after college instead and didn't seem too bothered by the break-up. He was never in when Mum got home – it was always Ginger. This made Ginger angry at times. Furthermore, Alex didn't have to worry; she was busy learning Chaucer and getting drunk in the Student Union.

Sometimes, Ginger wondered if she'd been an accident. What had made her parents decide to have a third child after all those years? She'd once asked Dad and he'd said that it was something to do with the economy. There hadn't been much to do that winter.

Soon, the house filled with the delicious aroma of biscuits spiced with nutmeg. As they cooled, Ginger got dressed, feeling inexplicably excited about seeing Dad, and also the imminent return of Alex from university. There wasn't much she could do to fix things with Frances today and it was kind of pretty outside. Frances and she would work things out. They always had.

Winter was Ginger's favourite time of year – she decided as she squeezed her enormous hair into a soft beanie hat. It gave you all sorts of excuses to wear lots of things that covered up the bits you didn't like. Hats especially came in handy. They could disguise even the most tragic victim of frizzy hair.

She was smiling when she left the house. However, her mood took a turn for the worse when she got in the car and found that it had been infiltrated by a strange life form.

"Ginger, this is Sonia. Sonia's a pharmacist," Dad spluttered nervously, as if that explained it. Ginger blinked hard and tried to make sense of the situation. Being sarcastic seemed like the best option.

"Oh, well, well. I do feel like I've got a headache. Does she have some paracetamol on her?" Ginger enquired, staring at the woman who was occupying the back seat.

The woman, Sonia, was taking up around four centimetres of the back of the car, so thin were her legs despite the wintery layers. On closer inspection, Ginger noticed that the layers were in a very fashionable shade of grey and her wool coat looked like one she had admired herself in Topshop. Her hair was cut in a swishy black bob, a million miles from Mum's permanent light brown fuzz fest. On even closer inspection, she noticed that Sonia was... young. Very young. Not college student young but well... too young for Dad. Ginger felt her temperature rising with anger and confusion.

"You can talk directly to Sonia, Ginger. She isn't deaf."

"Well I must be," retorted Ginger, not sure whether or not to fasten her seat belt or go back into the house, "... because I've never heard you mention a 'Sonia'."

"No, well..."

"Look, Ginger, it is lovely to meet you but I shouldn't have come..." said Minnie Mouse. Minnie Mouse? The noise that came out of Sonia's mouth was a high pitched squeak! It appeared that Dad had chosen to spend his time with a cartoon rodent. In spite of herself, Ginger burst out laughing. Sonia looked confused and hurt.

"No, no, of course you should!" argued Dad, totally ignoring the fact that his girlfriend had the most embarrassing voice in the world. "Ginger just needs to get to know you. It's my fault – I shouldn't have sprung this on you love…. What's so funny?"

Looking from one adult to the other, Ginger tried to make sense of the facts. Firstly, she was sitting in a car with Mickey's girlfriend who also happened to be her Dad's. Secondly, she had not been prepared in any way for this turn of events. If it wasn't for the fact that the situation was so unexpectedly hilarious, she would have cried. OMG, she thought to herself – as if things couldn't get worse. Ginger's head felt heavy all of a sudden and she concentrated on a leaf that was being swept around in a little tempest on the car bonnet.

"Ginger, say something, please," begged Dad.

"I'm sorry, Dad, I'm not doing this today," she eventually said and without a second look at the inhabitants of the small car, she collected her bag and climbed out.

Her father watched her go and wondered whether or not to follow but decided that an argument inside, probably with her mother present, was not the best course of action.

Ginger heard the car pull away and went straight upstairs to her bedroom and took out her homework.

"Love?" came her mother's voice from beyond the door, after a matter of seconds. "I heard you come back in. Is everything okay?"

"Fine," responded Ginger, her voice slightly cracking but as normal as she could manage.

"Ok, then. I'll be in the kitchen," said her mother, sounding concerned. Ginger guessed that Mum would go and call Dad immediately to find out what had happened. Just as she was trying to lose herself in a colour key of a map of the United Kingdom, her mobile phone beeped. It was Dad: I LOVE YOU, GINGER XXX.

*What do these people want from me?* thought Ginger. *They make us miserable when they're together and when they split up, they expect us to fit into their new lives with Disney characters and not kick up a fuss! Not a word of warning!*

Anger began to warm her cold cheeks again as she threw a felt tip across the room. It hit the wall above her bed, the lid flying one way, the marker the other. Unsure of what to do next, she went to her Mum's room to get the house phone to call Alex. But on the line she heard Mum's voice quietly swearing at someone. Presumably Dad. The words were threatening and entirely unlike any she's heard her mother use before. Ginger carefully hung the phone back up and went back to her room. *I don't know these people*, she thought to herself. *They are strangers*. Longing for her brother and sister to come home and tell her how to feel, she climbed into bed with her favourite old ted, Austin, and fell asleep sucking hard on her thumb.

She was woken by a hand gently stroking her face. It felt cool and soft and Ginger momentarily thought that she was small again. But then she realised she knew words like 'contemporary' and 'onomatopoeia' and that she didn't like watching *Animals Do the Funniest Things* anymore.

It was Alex wearing a gigantic wool scarf wrapped around her head at least fourteen times and a big smile.

"Hey, Ginger. How's you?" she asked softly.

"Been better," responded Ginger, her throat fuzzy with sleep.

"I heard all about it. What was she like?"

"Minnie Mouse," was all Ginger could manage.

"Minnie Mouse?"

"She sounds like flipping Minnie Mouse! But with that Topshop coat *I* wanted."

"The one with the hood and the furry collar?"

"Yes," replied Ginger, wondering why, out of all the irritating things about the day so far, the coat issue upset her the most.

"Did she seem nice?"

"Dunno," Ginger answered, pulling herself up on the bed with a yawn and that uncomfortable feeling one has when waking fully dressed in the afternoon.

"He told me about her a bit," confessed Alex, unravelling her scarf and placing it on the duvet. "He said they were very happy. I don't know what to think or say."

"No, neither do I. Do you think it's serious?" Ginger asked, knowing the answer was as clear as the flashing neon greetings attached to Frances' exterior walls.

"Yes. He said so. He's taking me out to dinner on Wednesday to get to know her. I haven't decided whether or not to go. How's Mum and Adam doing?"

Ginger climbed out of bed and looked in the mirror to examine the pillow scars on her face. "Ok, I guess. Mum seems better. Sometimes she's down. She's been cleaning and baking today, whatever that means. Probably, she's losing her mind. Adam's just the same. He doesn't seem bothered by anything apart from his new girlfriend. Love is in the air, I guess," Ginger concluded, slightly put out that SHE was the only one who didn't seem to be under Cupid's spell at the moment.

"Well, we knew there was someone else. Perhaps Sonia will turn out okay. Dad seems really happy with her."

Silently, the sisters shared a moment of reflection.

Then Alex jumped up and struck a duck-face pose.

"Let's go see Mum. I've got loads to tell you both!"

The evening unfolded without reference to Minnie Mouse, Dad or the weird thing Mum had done with her eyeliner. Mum had made a roast chicken for dinner and they enjoyed each other's company and the change that Alex's presence had brought to the house. Two became three and eventually, when Adam turned up, all four sat down to watch the *X-Factor* final. Bets were placed on who would win using chocolate raisins. Mum and Alex drank sherry, Adam did impressions of Simon Cowell and Cheryl Cole and Ginger snuggled up on the sofa in her favourite pyjamas, feeling like, for this one evening at least, the house was a home again.

At school, there was a lot of talk about a party. The party was being held by Hermione Higginbottom who was hardly the disco but nevertheless had very generous parents who tended to go out and leave her at home with instructions to enjoy herself and have some friends over. It could have been an axe-murderer who had an empty house and the pupils of Atherton Academy would have shown up in new high-tops and mascara.

The first she heard of it was when she caught Hermione squashed in a corner by Stephanie and Lydia next to the water fountain.

"Oh Hermione, you are so funny. We will have a totes amaze time. Shall I bring some part-poppers?" asked Stephanie, practically oozing fake interest.

"Huh, yeah, if you like?" replied Hermione, wiping the water she had been drinking away from her lips.

Ginger wondered if her invitation had got lost in the post. After all, she had been friends with Hermione since reception. Did people actually ever send invitations in the post?

The buzz around the party was everywhere. She even heard Milo admit that he might swing by if his Dad wasn't taking him out.

Ginger wondered whether she wanted to go to the party. It would be awful, she guessed. It was the kind of thing that her and Frances would have got ready for together, just like the prom... oh, but she hadn't gone to the prom, had she? Well, maybe this would be a chance for them to get dressed up and have some fun. It was the first party of high school after all!

When it became clear that she wasn't going to be invited, she manufactured a reason to work with Hermione in a performing arts lesson. She would ask her about it casually.

"Yeah, it is going to be awesome," admitted Hermione, stuffing a Snickers bar into her mouth between drama games.

"I would LOVE you to be coming. I'm really sorry to hear that you can't"

"What do you mean?!" Ginger asked angrily, forgetting that at that moment she should have been creating a 'C' shape with her body.

"Frances told me. About your ear-infection? That it is really bad and you can't stand loud music? It could be REALLY loud. I just got the new Mickey Mouse Club House Christmas CD! It is going to be crazy!"

"Oh yeah," said Ginger, feeling a sting. "I have got a bad ear-infection. It was nice of Frances to tell you."

"Such a shame. We'll be sure to tell you all about it after though."

Hermione finished her Snickers bar and got into a 'M' shape that looked very uncomfortable.

Ginger didn't even speak to Tom about what had happened. He hadn't been invited either. Yet, at the exact time the party started he texted her a picture he had taken of something funny he had seen on the road that day. He wasn't to know that her phone didn't receive images but the thought was there.

On Christmas Eve there was a knock at the door. Ginger opened it to find Frances' Mum. She was called Julie and had exactly the same face as Frances, only a bit chubbier around the edges. Ginger had always liked Julie. She was probably the Mum she should have had – all soft lines and giggles. She was friendly enough with Ginger's Mum but they didn't have much in common so never got together for more than a polite chat.

"Hi, Ginger, merry Christmas."

Frances's Mum looked down at a box she was holding. It was beautifully wrapped in golden paper with purple stars glittering under the porch lamp.

"This is for you, from Frances."

Thoughts flooded Ginger's mind too quickly and she struggled to know what to say. She couldn't understand why Julie was there with the present and she certainly didn't have a present to offer in return. She just didn't know what had happened, what had gone wrong, who was to blame or how it would end.

"Frances bought it months ago. She was too shy to bring it over herself. I don't know what's going on between you two but it isn't making either of you very happy by the looks of it. Friendship is so important and yours is so special."

Julie handed over the parcel and Ginger gingerly received it.

It took until ten o'clock on Christmas Day for Ginger to finally unwrap the gift. Normally Ginger took as much time over removing the paper as she did enjoying a gift; she loved the care that people took over wrapping gifts, the crisp, sparkly paper. But somehow, she thought she might give up half way if she did that.

Inside was a box made out of felt, in the style of a treasure chest. The lid was stuck down with Velcro and gave a satisfying zip noise when she pulled it apart.

Three small figures made of plastic were lazing around

at the bottom. One was a tiny witch with striped socks and a pointy hat. The other two were miniature princesses. One was smaller with a tiara and black hair flowing down her back. The other was taller with wild curly hair, a purple dress and a bored looking expression on her face.

"Princesses get chased by witch..." smiled Ginger, placing all three figures carefully under her pillow. Perhaps Frances was still her best friend, in spite of behaving in a way that was totally not cool. Ginger wondered whether she could find something that Frances would like in return but then remembered that Frances hadn't recently bought the present; it had been months ago. Would she have bought her a present now? Ginger was sure that she wouldn't have done. Maybe there was still a glimmer of hope that Frances would be her BFF again but Ginger didn't know how to make that happen. There was too much other stuff to worry about. A small part of Ginger wondered whether it would all be easier if Frances knew the truth but had no idea how to say the words she thought might need to be said. There were A LOT of New Year's resolutions to be made, she thought as she turned the light off and rolled over.

# January

### Bullying – Pupil Voice

Name: Ginger Mclean.

*Do you feel safe in school?*

Yes. All the time. It is perfect. I love it.

*Do you use social media sites like Facebook and Twitter?*

No. They are for people who don't have real friends. I have loads. Also, they are dangerous and full of weird men in trench coats pretending to be 12-year-old girls.

*Do you know what bullying is?*

Yes. I learned about it on EastEnders and in Year 5 through the medium of puppets.

*Have you ever seen any bullying in this school?*

No. We all get along just fine, thank you.

*Do you know anyone who is being bullied?*

No. See above.

*Do you know what to do if you are being bullied?*

Yes. I would go to tell a trusted adult immediately and probably start a support group for other victims. I am not a victim. But this is what I would do if I were. Which I'm not.

At first, the rumours were just stupid. A chunky blonde Year 8 girl called Sasha stopped Ginger on the Modern Foreign Languages Corridor and asked her if she was the girl who had to use a special medical formulation of deodorant because she suffered so badly from body odour. Ginger saw that the girl actually looked concerned and so, assuming that it was a case of mistaken identity, simply said 'Urm, no. But thank you for asking,' before rushing into French and getting on with the starter activity.

That was three days into the new term.

Towards the end of the week, she had been asked the same question by a couple more kids from her own year, plus she had been called 'Sweaty Mclean' in passing by a Year 9 boy she didn't recognise as she stood in the lunch queue pondering pizza or pasta.

The following Monday, her Maths teacher, Mr Jessop, took her aside and told her that if she needed to talk to anyone, there was a school counselling service that might help. Ginger had no idea what Mr Jessop was talking about and so just said, 'Urm, thank you. I'll bear that in mind.'

Tom had reluctantly confirmed the rumour that was going around about her famously stinky armpits and so Ginger took the precaution of wearing extra roll-on for the next few days and tried to avoid being paranoid about it.

Still, Ginger could only smell a rat.

Next, Tom told her that he'd heard Abigail Tatterton whispering to Chantel Peace about something she'd heard from her cousin Alfie's best friend, Andrew Rogers. Apparently, Ginger was moving schools because her parents were getting divorced and Ginger had to go to live in Bradford with her Mum and new stepfather. Tom was actually worried that the rumour was true and it took Ginger some time to convince him that it was a load of rubbish and that she wasn't going anywhere.

However, whereas the sweat rumour was embarrassing, the parent rumour gave her a bit of shock as she hadn't really told anyone about her parents' problems apart from Trevor and Tom, who seemed only vaguely interested in the story. How could anyone know? And the bit about moving to Bradford? Could she trust Tom? Yes, of course she could.

It was just plain weird.

Soon, it felt to Ginger, like the whole school was talking about her, laughing behind her back and generally having a lot of fun at her expense. She became argumentative with her friends.

'Hey, Ginger, can you show me your DT homework so that I can copy it – I forgot all about it,' asked Rebecca one Wednesday at break. Rebecca was notorious for being disorganised about her homework and often asked Ginger to let her 'borrow' hers.

'No. Do your own. Why should I slog over stupid research tasks on the internet so you can steal it? I'm not doing it anymore!'

'Durrh, because you like doing internet stuff and I don't,' responded Rebecca, as if it was a perfectly reasonable explanation.

'Maybe if you didn't spend all your time thinking about

your hair you'd be able to do it yourself,' Ginger almost shouted. Her body became full of rage and she actually felt like lashing out and hitting Rebecca over the head with her new Cath Kidston shopper.

*Thanks, Santa, for the weaponry.*

Instead, she just hurried away from the group and tripped up the stairs in front of a gang of Year 11s who laughed and pointed.

That night, a surprise arrived at the door.

It was Frances, visibly breathing hard as if she had run a marathon. She looked unwell and instead of her usual look of surprise, she looked cross.

"Is it true that you're moving to Bradford?"

Fighting back tears, Ginger said:

"Don't you think I'd have mentioned it, Franny? Of course not!" she'd not been able to look her friend in the eye as she said this, for fear of giving away any actual truths.

"Well it would be hard for you to mention it because we never speak to each other anymore. Where's your Dad, then, Ginger?" asked Frances, accusingly.

"Oh, er, he's been working away a lot."

"No he hasn't, Ginger. Teachers don't work away, anyway. Mum told me. He's left your Mum and you didn't even tell me." Frances stepped into the kitchen removing her coat and gloves.

Ginger concentrated on making a cheese and pickle sandwich and didn't answer. Again, something sharp stung the backs of her eyes.

"We were supposed to be best friends. I know you have had a hard time at school but I feel like I'm invisible to you. It's always about you – what you want to talk about and what you don't talk about."

Ginger's entire body was shaking as she picked up the knife to slice the bread.

"Well what about you?" Ginger screamed. "You have changed so much that I don't even know who you are anymore. Look at your hair! Do you even care about dogs anymore? I bet there are starving canines all over the country since you started being PLASTIC!"

Frances was clearly shaking as much as Ginger.

"I am not plastic," she spluttered, smoothing her hair as she spoke. "I just got on with being at high school. I tried to fit in and look, I have friends and you don't!"

"That's not true. I have friends. You even sent me a Christmas present. Deep down you miss me."

"That's true. I do miss you. But I don't miss being the one who has to listen all the time. You talk about me changing but it is you that needs to change. Perhaps then you can say we're friends but for now... well I'm quite happy with what I've got."

Frances began to put her winter layers back on. It went badly because her fingers were trembling so much. Wearing her gloves on the wrong fingers and with her hat on inside out she made to leave.

"See you later, Ginger. I'm going to meet Tom and Rebecca. We're going to hang out at the rec. And you may as well throw your present in the bin because we WILL NOT be playing „Princesses get chased by witch" EVER again."

Still Ginger refused to look up from her sandwich. The back door slammed as Frances left creating a vacuum of cold air. As she tried to cut the sandwich in half, the bread tore. Still shaking, she threw the sandwich at the kitchen window and went upstairs to bed.

Her bedroom felt like her prison these days. She spent more and more time in it and less and less in the rest of the house. Since Alex had gone back to university, she had felt a loneliness weighing down on her like an overladen rucksack she couldn't get off. Her thoughts seemed to be encased in lead – they were trapped inside her head and she felt there was no way of letting them out. She couldn't talk to anyone apart from Alex and Alex was far away, getting on with her own life as an adult. Ginger envied her – if she was a grown-up, nothing would matter so much.

Her body felt hot suddenly and her head ached. Mum was at her new evening class so she couldn't shout down for her to bring some paracetamol and a cup of tea. Adam was in his room, moshing around to some heavy metal music by the sound of it. Every now and then she heard a bang or a clatter as he knocked something off a shelf.

*What's the point?* She asked herself. *Everyone hates me. I'm stupid and ugly and even my parents don't care! Nobody would miss me if I wasn't here!*

When Mum finally came home she wasn't alone. Ginger could hear a man's voice in the kitchen between the door shutting, the whizz of the kettle boiling and the sound of mumbled discussion on the radio.

For a moment, Ginger thought it must be Dad and so she got out of bed and was heading down the stairs before she realised, too late, that the voice had a Scottish quality to it that certainly wasn't her father's.

'Ginger? Is that you?' called Mum, sounding giddy and nervous. 'Come and meet Robin.'

Ginger appeared at the threshold of the kitchen door to find her Mum giggling at the breakfast bar as if she had just heard the funniest joke ever.

Robin – whoever he was – turned to smile at Ginger. Ginger looked into his eyes and realised that he wasn't here to read the electricity metre. He was interested in Mum and she was interested in him.

Ginger's shoulders must have sunk even lower as Mum began to introduce the tall man with the thick glasses and shaved head, because a look of worry and regret swept across her face and she stopped talking.

Ginger managed a 'hi' and then retreated back to her room where she might be alone, but at least she wasn't going to have to deal with any more people.

She looked at Trevor and Trevor looked back at her, knowingly. Trevor yawned and it looked as though she would split in two. Ginger took the hint and got back into bed.

At orchestra practice, the following night, Ginger was all over the place, making silly mistakes which made the entire orchestra have to stop every five minutes to recover. She was getting dirty looks. Even Hermione Higginbottom, the weakest member of the group and unfortunate player of the timpani, looked exasperated and huffy.

Ginger kept her eyes on the music and her face unreadable.

Eventually, Mr Arnold told them to take a break and went off to make himself a cup of tea.

Musicians milled around, chatting and generally being silly. Ginger got out her resin and vigorously polished the strings on her bow in an attempt to look busy and aloof.

'You're going to break that,' said a voice, and Ginger's stomach churned.

Milo sat down next to her.

'I heard your parents are splitting up and you're moving to Bradford...'

'Well, don't believe everything you're told. Hmm, pass me that duster will you, please?' Ginger kept her eyes on her equipment and for once, felt that she didn't care much about whether she had a bogie or that her hair had undone itself from the tight ponytail she'd constructed before breakfast.

'My parents are divorced, you know,' continued Milo, ignoring the signals Ginger was sending out. 'They split when I was eight. It was hard. I know how you feel.'

'Nobody knows how I feel,' Ginger replied, before realising she was admitting that there was truth in the rumour. 'Who told you, anyway?' She couldn't help asking.

'I heard it from Stephanie Sykes.'

Suddenly, the rat had a name. She'd suspected as much.

'Well, I'm not going to Bradford. That's rubbish.'

'I thought it was mean of Steph to tell people that. I told her I thought so.' Milo continued lightly, as if he and 'Steph' were great friends.

'Thanks,' said Ginger, grudgingly but also grateful.

Mr Arnold came back and everyone calmed down and returned to their seats and instruments. He suggested they work on the new number they had been learning, a Beatles song that sounded great when he played it on the piano, but somehow awful when the members of Atherton Academy Orchestra got their hands on it.

It was in PSCHE a week later with Mrs Masterson that Ginger nearly gave in.

Having endured a week of sniggers from older pupils, more rumours about her ranging from 'Is it true that you wear giant nappies when you go to bed because you still wet it?' to 'Do you really get all your clothes from charity shops because your parents are drug addicts and can't afford to clothe you *and* buy their drugs?'

The topic of the lesson was bullying and Mrs Masterson had put them into groups to talk about their experiences. Obviously, Ginger was in a group with Milo, Tom, Brittany and, of course, Stephanie Sykes who had recently become determined to be known exclusively as 'Steph'.

The first thing they had to do was complete a questionnaire. Ginger completed it in purple gel pen and tried to be honest.

She noticed that Brittany wasn't even attempting her questionnaire but had managed to draw a rather lovely scene where an evil looking elf was beating a fairy with a mushroom stalk. She supposed that did show something of the world of bullies.

They sat around the two tables that had been joined together in silence. Tom leant back in his chair and began humming some dance tune under his breath and looking out of the window. Stephanie had her elbows on the table and took hold of the fat marker pen and sugar paper that they were to use to create a 'brain-storm' of their ideas. Milo and Arron were talking in low voices about a football match they'd seen at the weekend. Ginger chewed her nails and tried not to tremble.

Business like and bossy, Stephanie began to talk about her experiences of bullying, as Ginger was reminded of those dreadful teenagers on the TV show, *Young Apprentice*. Mum always said that if any of those kids were hers, she'd try to lose them in the supermarket.

'I once had a terrible experience of bullying,' announced Stephanie and, in all fairness, this got the attention of the rest of the group. All eyes focussed on her. She looked as though she was about to say something that was very painful to her, but also, slightly pleased with herself.

'Yes, it hurts to talk about it...but... once, when I was out shopping with Lydia...' she stopped to dab her eyes with a tissue, 'and I tried this pink jumpsuit on and she said... she said... she said I looked like Peppa Pig after too many pig treats.'

Stephanie put her face in her hands and fell silent as the rest of the group looked on amazed.

There was nothing anyone could think of to say until Tom broke the silence with a loud laugh – one of those that actually starts with 'Ha!' and then turns into a sort of wheezing noise as the air runs out.

"Okay, Steph, thanks for that," Mrs Masterson said quickly, shooting Tom a disapproving look whilst clearly hiding a smirk of her own behind manicured fingers.

"Actually," said Tom, "I know someone who is being bullied right now, in this fine educational establishment and it isn't because she looks like Peppa Pig."

Ginger's heart jumped into her throat. *He wouldn't, would he?*

Of course, this was Tom and if there was one thing he could be relied up on to do, as well as look great in high tops, it was that he would tell the truth.

OMG.

"Yes, my friend has had rumours made up about her. Things that are rubbish and hurtful."

He glanced at her.

"Him, I mean."

Mrs Masterson put her pen to her mouth and leaned in. Stephanie's eyes lit up and Milo crossed his legs awkwardly.

What would he say next?

"In fact, some of these rumours are so bad that I know she feels that she has no friends, but she's wrong."

"He, he means." I said, shooting him poo-eye.

"Some of this has even been done on the internet. On Facebook."

This was news to Ginger. She didn't have a Facebook account. She didn't have a smart phone to get one and Mum had a thing about social media sites. Mum said they were the devil.

"What has your friend done about the problem?" asked Stephanie, barely containing her sense of pride.

"I don't know, Stephanie," said Tom. "She just seems to be putting up with it because she knows that the person behind the rumours is definitely a loser and probably very, very, deeply pathetic. Not to mention weird looking."

"Tom, that has nothing to do with it. However, I am concerned for your friend. So guys, what can Tom's friend do to solve the problem and stop the bullies?"

Milo put his hand up.

"She needs to tell a teacher. Then she needs to stop listening to the gossips because they are idiots and she is better than all of them. Sorry, I mean *he*."

Ginger froze.

Stephanie's eyes began to gleam with wet tears.

Tom chewed on a hang nail and nodded his head.

"Okay, I think that's good advice. Tell your friend that he or she needs to talk to me or another adult in school very soon. Bullies need to be dealt with quickly. But remember, bullies are usually people who are feeling bad about themselves for some reason."

Ginger was not sure who was suffering more: her or Stephanie. An emotion passed through her veins and she wasn't sure whether it was happiness or sadness.

When the bell went, Stephanie went out on her own, not bothering to wait for her pack of duck-faced clones.

Milo hung back and spoke quietly to Mrs Masterson whilst Tom and Ginger packed their things together in silence.

"I'm sorry, Ginge," said Tom.

"I know," replied Ginger, not knowing how to feel.

"You've got to talk to someone."

Suddenly, Mrs Masterson turned to face them.

"Ginger, can you hang back for a moment, please?"

"Sorry Miss, I have to go to the... the toilet."

"Okay, well if you do need to talk to anyone honestly, please do come to me. These things can get worse very quickly if you don't deal with them."

One of the reasons that Ginger looked forward to university was that there seemed to be an awful lot of time to not do much but be cool and hang out with like-minded friends. She pictured herself aged nineteen in a fashionable café discussing who would win a fight between the Gorgon Medusa and a Cyclops or who Harry Potter should really have married. She never actually saw Alex doing this but she did appreciate that when Alex got a holiday she really did get a holiday.

It was well into January and she was still at home.

They had agreed to go shopping one Saturday afternoon in town and were busy talking all the way on the bus about whether they would rather meet a Cyclops, the Minotaur or the Gorgon Medusa in a dark alley. Ginger thought she would definitely rather meet the Cyclops. Alex fancied her chances against the Minotaur.

Alex had got a new boyfriend and she was busy describing him over the hanging rails of clothes in the shops.

"He's got a bit of beard, I suppose. But that's quite a good thing, I think."

"Urrrghh," shouted Ginger over the loud music playing in the store. All she could think about was how Mr Pearson had recently grown a beard and that it made him look like Mr Twit. She had seen something move in it twice.

"Oh, I like beards. All the interesting boys at uni have them. They are a bit strange when you kiss…"

"Urghh! Shut up, please! I'm going to be sick!"

"So tell me about who you like. Didn't you used to like that boy with the unusual name…what's he called… Milo?"

Pretending to be fascinated by a pair of tights that seemingly cost £25, Ginger ignored her sister.

"Ah, so you still like him!"

Suddenly Alex was in her face, grinning from ear to ear.

"So how is he these days? Didn't you once say that he was the cleverest boy in your class? Is he still just clever or has he also started to be cute as well? Hmmm?"

"Oh, he's still around. I sit next to him a lot. He's still clever. That's it. We have to hang around sometimes together because we're both in the orchestra."

Alex looked at her with pleading puppy dog eyes, desperate for more information.

"Yes, he is still cute. But he'll never like me in that way. For the moment, I'm just delighted that I haven't made a total fool out of myself for a couple of weeks in front of him."

"Oh no, what have you done before?"

Ginger told Alex about her disasters in romance over a cup of hot chocolate in Costa. It had never really occurred to Ginger that what she had with Milo was a romance, but she quite liked telling someone about her feelings at last. It was a weight off her mind and, actually, fairly good fun.

The shopping trip lasted for nearly seven hours though both girls returned home with only a couple of small bags from Superdrug.

Sitting at the back of the bus, squeezed between two old ladies who spoke over the top of them about the good old days, Ginger asked Alex whether she had been happy in Year 7.

"No! It was awful. There were these Year 9 girls who made my life hell. Sometimes, they waited for me after school and shouted names at me. Once, one of them took my bag and emptied it in the bin. Another time, one of them punched me!"

"What did you do?"

"I told Mum about it and she went in to school to talk to my teacher. But that was a long time after it had started. It helped a bit, I guess. I'm glad I did.

"Did you really do that or are you just saying it because it is what you should have done?" asked Ginger, suspiciously.

"Yes, of course. If I hadn't, I think they'd still be waiting for me now outside university every afternoon!"

Alex squashed in closer to Ginger and further away from the old lady who was kindly reaching round to offer the other old lady a mint.

"Do you think that old ladies ever run out of mints?" she whispered.

Ginger didn't respond, lost in her own thoughts.

"Anyway, tell me more about that dreadful girl Stephanie Sykes. I love your stories about her!"

"Well," began Ginger, "last week she came to school with a story about meeting Justin Bieber at the swimming baths."

"No way! Genius…"

They arrived home howling with laughter and enjoying every minute of each other's company. Mum and Adam were in the kitchen arguing about what the unpleasant smell was coming from his bedroom. They both turned to Ginger and Alex aghast. Raucous laughter was rare in the Mclean house these days.

"What's got into you two? What on earth are you talking about?"

Alex and Ginger looked at each other, made zipping gestures across their mouths and fell into even more fits of giggles on the kitchen floor.

# February

*My Dearest Valentine by G. Mclean*
*Wasps are stripy,*
*Bees are buzzy,*
*I'll have a boyfriend*
*When my hair is less fuzzy.*

*Forget about the big 'V',* decided Ginger. *Valentine is for losers and big card shops hell-bent on squeezing pocket money out of lonely people. Not people like me who have options and a Level 6A in Reading and common sense. Ha, in your face St Valentine! I will not be a slave to your cruel joke.*

Anyway, the 6th was her birthday and all Ginger wanted to do was go into town and spend her Topshop vouchers on some new jeans. This was not just a luxury item. Over the last six months, Ginger had grown by another two inches and was now looking down on most Year 10s in school and also her Mum. Her sweaters and t-shirts had begun to look like they were made for the younger sister of an Oompa Loompa. Her trousers were practically skimming the top of her ankles and it was cold outside. She suffered constantly from goose-bumps and this did nothing if not emphasise the tiny hairs on her legs.

She had thought long and hard about whether or not to shave them like Mum did but had decided that if nothing else, the hairs provided an extra layer of warmth. Just as the goddesses had intended.

Instead of replenishing her wardrobe with things that fitted, she was constantly being taken out by Dad to somewhere boring. They would exchange awkward updates on work and school, discuss the weather and what TV shows they had watched that week.

Neither of them would mention Minnie (who Dad insisted was called Sonia).

Nor would Robin be mentioned (who Mum insisted on

calling darling).

When the car beeped outside, Ginger braced herself for another hour of fun but when she got into the car complaining that she really needed to go to town, she nearly fell back out when the voice that returned her not-so-warm-greeting sounded suspiciously Disney-esque.

It was only Minnie Mouse herself.

Sitting in the driver's seat.

As if it were her car.

Ginger felt something uncomfortable under her bum and looked down to discover that she was sitting on a parcel.

"Oh," was all that she could manage.

"Hi, Ginger. I bet you're not in the least bit pleased to see me but your Dad has been held up. He put his back out running and sent me to give you your present."

Ginger was aghast for many reasons. Not least because she had just learned that her father had been running. She wondered why she hadn't been informed of this earlier. She checked her phone to see if she had received a text. It confirmed the worst.

"SORRY GINGER. IN PAIN. HAPPY BIRTHDAY. I LOVE YOU. XXX"

"Running?"

"Erm, yes. He's been doing it for a few weeks. He's trying to lose weight and drink less. He's doing really well. Until now, that is."

It was both the best news she had heard for ages and also the worst. Was she really expected to accept some hopeless attempt at a present from Minnie and say thank you?

"Open the present now. If you like. I chose it."

Ginger had no choice. She hadn't been brought up to be rude and although the parcel was bound to contain something an eight-year-old might have enjoyed in 1970, she could hardly just run away this time.

Tentatively, she unwrapped the parcel. It contained a really nice rucksack, covered in stars. She had seen it before in River Island and liked it a lot. There was also a Topshop voucher in a small envelope that fell on the car floor as she shook off the wrapping.

In spite of herself, Ginger was impressed.

"Your Dad said it was your favourite shop," said Minnie hurriedly, which made her sound like she'd just taken another hit on the helium balloon she must keep in her handbag.

"Er, yes. Thanks."

"We could go into town and spend it? If, er, you like?"

The offer was tempting in many ways; the warm car was loads more appealing than the bus.

But it wasn't right. She would go to town on her own, or with Mum. Not this strange voiced imposter with her good taste and irritatingly kind offer.

"Some other time, eh?" said Ginger, avoiding eye contact.

"Yes, Ginger. I would like that. Some other time."

And Ginger got out of the car, taking care not to slam it too hard.

Inside, Mum was talking to Robin on the phone but,

when Ginger came back in, she made to leave the kitchen. She had confusion on her face but Ginger knew well enough to leave it alone.

The time she had spent with Alex had made her feel a bit stronger; it was like Alex possessed a magical skill to make her feel that anything was possible.

Something had been bubbling in her mind all afternoon and she decided that it was time to fix things with Frances.

Ginger phoned her and got her on the third ring. Frances sounded busy and flustered, as if she hadn't looked at the caller ID.

Through the bad reception, Ginger could hear a voice in the background asking Frances who was on the line.

The voice was clearly Stephanie Sykes'.

Stephanie Sykes was friends with her Frances.

Frances was with Stephanie Sykes!

Ginger's mouth formed the shape of an O. O for OMG.

If this was how birthdays were going to pan out from twelve onwards, Ginger decided that she'd had enough.

She hung up, before Frances had even managed to force any kind of conversation.

It was over.

Ginger thought back over the years to the fun they'd had... Dressing up in their Mum's clothes when they were six, selling rose-water perfume from the end of their driveways, Frances' granddad going nuts when he realised that his prize roses were now mush in jam jars... When they'd both chosen the exact same party dresses to go to Hermione's pizza and karaoke eighth birthday party and then pretended they were sisters for five months. When they'd both first read *Harry Potter and the Philosopher's Stone* and swore to only go to Hogwarts if the other got in too.

But they hadn't got the letter at the end of Year 6. They'd both ended up at Atherton. They hadn't gone to Diagon Alley shopping for a new wand but Frances certainly had something new... A shiny new friend.

She knew that she should've seen this coming. 'Foreshadowing' is what it's called when a writer gives hints early on in a novel. Her life was now a tragic story and coming over all *Tracy Beaker*.

Although Stephanie had laid off the rumour-mill since January, all was not forgiven and never would be. Ginger was fairly sure that someone had tipped off Mrs Masterson and she had dealt with it with a snap of her red talons and a few cool threats. Still, whatever happened, Ginger was relieved. It was enough to be a heroine in the novel of her own life.

Pulling herself together, Ginger found her Mum in the hall, tidying up shoes. Carefully, her Mum gave her a warm cuddle, pulling Ginger close into her chest that always smelled faintly of vinegar and Dove, in a good way.

"You want to go and spend those vouchers?"

"Yep. That would be nice."

Ginger and her Mum shopped for three hours before hitting Wagamamas. In Topshop, her Mum had even picked out some clothes to try on to keep her company in the changing rooms. Ginger laughed as her Mum tried to squeeze into a pair of size 10 high-waisted shorts.

Over their noodles, the girls chatted about Alex and Adam and then about Minnie. It was the first time.

"Maybe you should at least try to get to know her. If your Dad likes her, then maybe she is okay. He has good taste in women, if nothing else!"

"Well he's started running, so clearly he's going mad."

"Running? Whatever next. You know, it is a mid-life crisis. For both of us. Life is too short to be only a bit happy. And it has nothing to do with you. Do you believe that?"

Her Mum started looking at Ginger carefully and she remembered how Mums can see into your very soul.

"I know that," Ginger said honestly.

"How's school? Tell me about it. How's Frances? I haven't seen her for ages."

"Things are good," Ginger said again, hoping that her recent lying streak was coming to an end tomorrow. It was exhausting. Before you could say Pad Thai, Ginger had told her Mum all about the last few months and how great they'd been. The chilli made her sniff quite a lot through her words but it felt good making her Mum happy.

"That's just great," her Mum said, pushing her food around the plate. "I should have asked before."

"It isn't your fault. I'm a tricky one," replied Ginger through a mouthful of peanut.

But just then, she smiled.

It was a rare and wonderful moment of warmth between mother and daughter... One that could only lead to a bright new future of communication and understanding. Perhaps even one where they didn't have to tell each other fibs just to get through the day without disappointment.

However, the smile on her Mum's face began to dip at the edges and Ginger sensed that the moment was over. How right she was.

"Ginger, I've been meaning to say..." began her Mum, wielding a fork menacingly." I really think we need to get you to an orthodontist. Your teeth are a mess. Braces, I think."

Ginger's eyes bugged even further than normal as she then remembered that parents are like small children; you get their attention for five minutes and then they find something new that they want to wreck.

Later that night, Ginger received a text message from Frances. Well, she guessed it was from Frances, but actually she had deleted her from her phone so just a number appeared above the message.

I KNOW WE'RE NOT FRIENDS ANYMORE. BUT YOU SHOULD KNOW THAT STEPHANIE WON'T BE GIVING YOU ANY MORE TROUBLE. SHE IS OKAY REALLY. LATERS.

Something in her stomach made Ginger clutch it. It might have been that Frances hadn't used text speak. It could have been the Pad Tai but Ginger knew it wasn't.

It was guilt.

At the end of the half term, Ginger had been in a

particularly bad mood, this having been brought on by a particularly bad hair day and a spot on her chin.

Another reason for her awful mood was that she had received what she decided was absolutely a hoax Valentine's card. The card had appeared on her desk in a Maths lesson. She had got up to find a calculator that worked and returned to find it sitting upright in its envelope against her pencil case.

She shifted her eyes around to see who had seen it. Everyone was getting on with their multiplications, including Stephanie.

"Tom," she whispered.

"What? I always find these tricky. Help me will you, Ginger?"

"No, look! Who put that there?" her whisper was getting louder as she felt her face flush.

"I have no idea," said Tom, smiling but then looking back down to his work. "Maybe someone likes you and wanted to send you a Valentine's card, you idiot."

Ginger chose to ignore this possibility. It was bound to be a cruel joke. If it wasn't for the fact that her parents were far away at work she would have immediately suspected them. It was exactly the kind of thing they did when she was little.

However, on this occasion they had air-tight alibis.

She was just stuffing it into her bag and praying that nobody else had seen it when Milo arrived back at their desk.

"Couldn't find my book," he said by way of explanation.

"Ah! Super! I see you found it!" enthused Ginger.

Milo looked at her strangely and opened his text book.

"You are weird sometimes," he whispered, smiling to himself.

The card had been quite harmless. Cute even. However, there was clearly foul practice at work here and she seethed all week.

On Thursday, Ginger had been talking to Tom and some of his friends from Drama Club when an opportunity for revenge had arisen. They were all having a laugh about embarrassing things they'd done as kids. Tom had once told them that he wore a Spiderman mask and his sisters' gymnastics leotard for nearly a year. Even when his Mum managed to persuade him to wear other clothes, the leotard was underneath and the mask stayed on. Ginger had begun to feel much better about life and couldn't help thinking that her old head teacher had been SO wrong about her not being good at making friends.

So she had told them some much understated versions of a few of her lesser moments of calamity, enjoying how they hung on her every word because she was Tom's friend.

It didn't take long before she was holding court and telling tales about other school mates they all knew who had gone to Stanningate. Obviously, none of them were there to defend themselves. Ginger really couldn't help it when she had a stroke of genius.

"And I know it didn't happen at primary school but I do know something about someone we all know here... Someone with blonde hair and far too much lip-gloss..."

The drama nerds all began to nod and look very interested. No names were needed for them to guess who she was talking about. With barely a pang of guilt words began to fall out of Ginger's mouth...

"I heard she practises kissing on her dog..."

Before the words had formed into little whispers in the cold air, the drama geeks were rolling around laughing.

"She has a Chihuahua!" screamed Tom. "I've seen it!"

"Yes! I know!" screamed Ginger in return, only slightly amazed by the screechiness of her own voice and her ability to lie. "I saw her doing it at a sleepover a few months ago! She was all like..." and then Ginger launched into an Oscar-winning impersonation of someone French-kissing a small dog.

Tom suddenly looked a little less like he was enjoying the story and Ginger's palms began to sweat as she realised that only Tom would know that the likelihood of Ginger being invited to a sleepover at Stephanie's was as likely as her being invited to Kate and Will's for supper.

Only after the Drama Club members had dispersed, still laughing their loud stage-laughs and doing their own dog-snogging routines, did Tom tell her in a low voice that if that story was true, then he was going to make the school's elite rugby squad next term.

It was only a tiny bit noticeable that he had a look of quiet pride as he walked off to his art lesson in the lower block.

Ginger had forgotten all about it when she got home and found Robin in the kitchen with Mum.

Mum was wearing another tea-dress. It was like she'd got nothing to do all day but dress up like a domestic goddess. Clearly Robin had never tasted her lasagne if he was convinced by that.

"We're going out to that new Italian for dinner. Go and get changed, Ginger. No arguments; you're coming too."

"Aw, but…"

"GO!"

Ginger went upstairs and looked in her wardrobe. There were enough suitable outfits in there for a quick dinner at a restaurant but few of them fit. She looked nostalgically at all the pretty dresses she had worn for special events over the last couple of years. They were like precious diary entries marking birthdays and other happy times.

She decided that having been so clever and funny that day, she would go to dinner with Robin and Mum and be as vibrant and cheerful as she could manage. Robin didn't seem that bad really.

Over their starters, Mum and Robin told her about a film that had been to see together. Mum glowed as she remembered how the man sitting next to them had told them that he thought that there was too much swearing and violence in films these days but he liked to keep an eye on things in case they got too bad.

Ginger told them about how she had a new group of friends and would probably join the Drama Club.

"Oh, now that is a great idea," said Robin. "I had a lot of fun being in school productions. Of course, it was a brilliant way to meet girls…"

Mum jabbed him in the ribs and giggled.

Ginger felt a little uncomfortable. There was nothing more embarrassing than flirting adults, particularly when one of them was your mother.

The conversation soon turned to other things and Ginger found that it was not really very painful at all to have dinner with your Mum and her boyfriend. One day, she would perhaps marry some gorgeous young actor who she met on a film set. They would laugh about how she had been an ugly duckling with no friends at school before she found her true vocation and auditioned for a West End show. The rest would be history, probably made into a bio-movie with her starring as herself and him in the lead. Possibly as Tom, possibly as Milo.

Who knew? With things going better, the world was her oyster (as Gran used to say when she got her first Motability scooter).

# March

## Independent Research Project, Chapter 1
## My Top 5 Characters from Greek Mythology

*Pandora*

She looked in a box that sounded really fascinating. It was not a good idea, but still, who wouldn't have?

*Athena*

Goddess of intelligence, war and handicrafts. What a woman! Imagine being able to win a battle through amazing strategy whilst quilting a bed spread.

*Hermes*

God of sending messages and trickery. We could all learn a lot from him about how to handle our parents. He was also a God of athletics but we won't dwell on that.

*Poseidon*

God of the sea. Also, Percy Jackson's dad. He could create a flood whenever he needed one. How often do we all wish we could make a flood happen and get out of doing something we don't want to do? For instance, being back-stop in rounders.

*Persephone*

She was a bit silly really and caused all sorts of problems for her mother, however, she has the best name and you sound extremely clever if you can pronounce it correctly: *per-sef-on-y.*

Along with the tonsillitis epidemic that had cut down so many Year 7s since February half-term, social networking habits had spread amongst the Year 7s of Atherton High over the year like a plague. Facebook was the most popular, though Twitter and Instagram were fast catching up.

Ginger was not opposed to this movement. Alex was a keen Tweeter and often shared funny stories from celebrities with her when she was home. Adam was just as into it but fiercely private about what he spent all his time doing on his laptop in his stinky room. They both had their own iPhones too so there was hardly a waking moment when they weren't both thumbing away at glaring little screens and grunting whenever you asked them a question.

Needless to say, Mum was not impressed by any of this. Yet outrageously SHE spent her fair-share of time with her nose in her own selection of technology: her own PC, Kindle and phone.

"Mum, why has everyone in this family got something upon which to communicate with the world, whilst I have to rely on screaming into the trees and hoping a monkey passes on my inner most witty thoughts and observations?"

"Ginger, what on earth are you talking about?" said Mum without even looking up from her emails.

"Ah, perhaps I should email you instead. I'll just have a look to see if I can squash my hand-written notes into the CD-drive of your laptop, shall I?"

Mum looked up and smiled warily.

"You have a phone and I let you use the PC whenever you need it for homework. That's enough for you."

"I'm not so sure, Mum…"

Ginger produced what looked like a pirate treasure map from behind her back. The week before, she had carefully stained a piece of white A4 with tea and hidden it to dry in her wardrobe. Since then, she had used her best flowery joined-up handwriting to add to it a list of reasons why she at least deserved an iPhone. She hoped that this would underline her point that it was not acceptable to be as well-equipped as a 19<sup>th</sup> century chimney sweep.

*Dearest Mother,*

*I am writing this with a sanguine heart and faith in your compassion. Also, I was thinking how nice your eyes look since the daffodils have opened their yellow wings to embrace the new season. What follows is a list, though possibly not comprehensive (as there are many more good reasons), why I should be gifted an iPhone 5 or at the very least, a MacBook before I turn eighteen and am shunned from the modern world:*

> *1.  The educational benefits of internet mobile data are endless. Many teaching professionals have referred to this in my presence and I suspect that they are implying that I will one day fail all my GCSEs without one;*

> *2.  I am a good daughter who rarely leaves a mess in the bathroom (unlike my male sibling*

*who we both know to be gross) and occasionally I am helpful and make you a cup of tea when I am making one for myself;*

*3. Dad would get me one if he were here and if you say 'no' then I'll be forced to go to him and ask for one. In broken homes, it is not uncommon for the father to make up for his absence with extravagant and / or extremely necessary gifts.*

*4. My IT skills are woefully behind that of my peers who have constant access to the internet. I am scraping a Level 4B and some of them are on a 4A.*

*5. The dream I have of becoming an author/archaeologist/concert musician/presenter of Newsnight/Chief-in-Editor at Vogue is fairly unlikely to come true if I continue to live like Anne Frank, with nothing but a pencil and paper, cut off from the world.*

*6. Alex and Adam have iPhones.*

*All my love,*

*Ginger Mclean (your precious daughter)*

Mum was smiling as she read the script and made noises that Ginger felt were fairly condescending and uncalled for like 'ha!' and 'huh!' and then 'as if!'.

"Perhaps you can have a laptop but you will not be having a Facebook account. I've seen enough damage caused by that at work..." She adjusted her glasses and

Ginger knew she was inspecting her overbite as much as she was thinking about whether to allow her daughter to join the technical revolution. "I'll see if Robin can fix an old one up for you. He's really good at that."

"No, Mum, that won't do. I'm already a social outcast because you passed on your stupid hair genes! And the phone I have is not acceptable. Did you know that in order to power it I have to get Trevor to pedal on her wheel fast every night?"

"Very funny. I'll think about it. Right after I've made you a dentist appointment."

Ginger slumped her shoulders and went off to her room where she half-heartedly tried out some verbs for her French homework and then watched a documentary about internet billionaires. Adam stuck his head in just as Bill Gates was telling her what qualities she needed to be disgustingly rich and successful herself.

"Seriously, Adam, you would think that with all that money he would get a personal stylist. Jeans and trainers! So Dad!"

"Yeah, well anyway, whatever..." said Adam, clearly not willing to engage in an interesting conversation with his little sister. "I wanted to show you something that made me laugh..."

Out of his hoody pocket (which was also full of bits of sticky-looking tissue) he produced his phone. Covering the screen he unlocked it, glancing suspiciously at Ginger every so often and then held it out proudly. "This is funny."

The screen was unmistakably Facebook. Even though

Ginger had probably only seen a Facebook page twice, she recognised the layout and blue banner.

Adam clicked a box and a picture filled up the screen. At first, she wasn't sure what it was and then as her brain made sense of the image, some sick came up into the back of her throat and she fell back on the bed.

Someone clever or mean - depending on how you looked at it – had used their wizardry to put Stephanie Sykes face next to a love heart and a Chihuahua. Underneath it rather unimaginatively said: 'I practise my kissing on my dog". The background was pink and the dog was wearing a diamond collar.

"Isn't she in your class at school? I think I remember her from your rubbish parties when you were little. It is so weird."

Was Adam friends with Stephanie on Facebook? Unlikely! She asked him, hoping that Stephanie had perhaps posted it herself in a moment of brilliant coincidence.

"No way! I'm NOT friends with little kids. Oh, Ginger, sweet sister, you are so naïve. Actually, I've no idea where it came from originally but I got it from Dougie Smith. Look..." he pointed to the bottom of the screen and Ginger felt even more queasy. "It's got 79 likes already."

Ginger grabbed the phone from Adam's unwilling hand and began to scroll down through the list of comments. They ranged from really mean to evil genius.

This did not feel good.

On the walk to school the next day, Ginger caught up with Frances and shyly offered her a Chewit. It was rare to see Frances walking. It was rare to see Frances up close these days. It had been months since they had really spoken.

Ginger was keen to tell Frances about how great her life was since she had begun hanging around with the drama crowd and at some point, she wanted to say thank you for the 'Princesses get chased by witch' figures. Even the ear-infection thing seemed like a decade ago.

Unable to refuse a sweet, Frances took one and unwrapped it. She hardly looked at Ginger as she did it, preferring to look at her phone screen.

Frances was looking good. She had continued to change shape and her uniform no longer looked like it belong to someone who was fifty centimetres taller and two dress sizes smaller. This along with the constant hair and face overs that Rebecca provided was making Frances stand out as one of the pretty girls. Ginger felt a pang of jealousy and pulled down her blazer slightly as it was riding up under her school coat.

Finally Frances spoke.

"Did you hear about Steph? She's so upset. I thought you might be pleased."

For many reasons, Ginger acted innocent. *No! She had not heard about Steph... She hoped that Steph was okay... She had always admired Steph's way with sequins...*

Frances looked at her in a puzzled way but continued to tell her what had happened. Some of this

Ginger knew but there was news. Stephanie was probably going to leave school. The IT support team were trying to get to the bottom of the bullying and someone was in big trouble.

"It really makes me sick. I'm never going on Facebook again. It is *so* 2012 anyway," concluded Frances.

As the girls continued to walk, Ginger felt that her knees would give way under her. After about five minutes, Frances was too busy checking her Facebook News Feed to notice that Ginger had fallen behind.

The toilet door slammed shut and Ginger sat on the seat whilst her trembling stopped. She was so wrapped up in her thoughts that she barely blinked when she heard Tom's voice from the other side of the door.

"This is AMAZEBALLS! The smell is... OMG, so... nice! And there's soap...!"

"Tom? Is that you? What the heck are you doing in the girls' toilets, you freak?!"

"Chill, babe, I sneaked in when I saw an opportunity. You better let me in before some Year 8 comes in to shovel on another ton of blusher."

Opening the door reluctantly, Ginger made Tom swear he wouldn't use the toilet whilst he was in there.

She landed back down on the toilet seat and began to cry. Before she knew it, she was pouring out every thought that she'd had over the last twenty four hours, many of which Tom found hilarious and some just plain hysterical.

"Look, will you just shut up. Keep your mouth closed

and act as if nothing has happened. You didn't know that Quentin was going to photo-shop that picture. You're not even cool enough to have a Facebook account. It will be okay."

"Quentin?" managed Ginger feebly through a snot bubble.

"Yes, the drama geek with the Simon Cowell trousers and the train-track teeth? He's also an IT geek. Shock!"

*It was possible that she wouldn't be found out,* thought Ginger carefully. A pesky voice in her head (that sounded a lot like Alex) kept saying '*Confess! Confess!*' but it was too much to bear. That would not be happening. Statistically, the chances of her being found out by IT technicians was unlikely whilst the chances of her being found out through confession was high. *Doh*, she thought, *no-brainer.*

They made it to English class on time and when Milo asked her if she was okay 'because her eyes looked a bit pink', she told him she was fine. Early hay fever.

On the other side of the classroom she noticed a glaringly empty chair. Steph 'Puppy Love' Sykes was not in school.

At home that night, Ginger paced her bedroom. She could sense that Tom was wrong. She could sense a disaster. Had she turned on the weather forecast, she suspected that the weatherman would predict a storm on the horizon: "Better hunker down, folks. This will be more than a spring shower."

Mum was busy arguing with Alex (who was home

again) about a credit card bill. Apparently money didn't grow on trees and Alex needed to be more responsible.

Adam was in his room playing on his Xbox at a volume that sounded like a world war was actually breaking out in there.

How could she think with all this noise!

At that moment the house phone started ringing. It was Dad. For her. Something about going to the seaside for the weekend.

Ginger said that she was too busy with erm, an RE project and could they rain-check until the summer (or when she was not having a crisis and probably about to be in the biggest trouble of her life).

Dad disappeared and the phone started ringing again.

This time it was Tom inviting her to a Drama Club audition. The part was perfect for her, he said. They needed someone who was tall enough to play an adult and she was the tallest person her knew.

"No, thank you!" screamed Ginger and slammed down the phone.

In order to calm down, she locked her bedroom door and took out her favourite note book. There was nothing better than making a list to make you feel less like running out into the rain naked and screaming 'why me' repeatedly at the Gods.

Firstly, she began a list of her favourite films. She tore that up after *The Nightmare before Christmas* and began a new list. Her favourite books! Of course. *Anne of Green Gables, The Twits, Percy Jackson, The Hunger Games,*

*Harry...* No! What was she doing! This was no time for literature.

What she needed to do was formulate a plan to prepare for the inevitable; a list of good reasons why she had sunk to such lows that would excuse all her wrong-doings.

*Reasons why I cannot be held responsible for my actions!*

*By Ginger Mclean*

*1. I am a child. I make mistakes. Remember how everyone laughed when I was learning to swim and couldn't and nearly drowned? You found that funny!*

*2. I come from a broken home. This has historically led to people doing all kinds of stupid things. Blame the parents!*

*3. I have tried in vain to live with a stupid name. You don't find girls called 'Sarah' and 'Jane' committing dreadful acts of revenge, do you?*

*4. I have bad hair. If I had been born with a shiny curtain of blonde, would I be so bitter?*

*5. I am too clever. It has been a burden for all. Even my Grandma used to say that I was too clever for my own good!*

*6. I was allowed to watch too much CBeebies when I was little. Often whilst eating chicken nuggets.*

Ginger put her pen down and drifted into a peaceful sleep, relieved that she had a plan and ready to face the consequences.

Considering that she had spent quite a lot of time in her educational life waiting for a technician to fix the computer she was expected to work on, they moved pretty quickly that week at Atherton. Jamal Jones, the new network support manager had taken pride in his speedy detective work and a name was placed on Mr Pearson's desk by the last Friday in March.

Quentin had inevitably been hauled in and squealed like a rat. Ginger doubted this was due to Mr Pearson having been trained by the Mafia to make people talk. Ginger pictured Quentin throwing his head back in his chair and confessing everything before Mr Pearson had even opened his mouth.

It would have only taken a moment of further enquiry before Quentin gave them Ginger's name, address and shoe size.

Sitting across from her now were Mr Pearson and Mrs Masterson and they did not look angry. That was the scariest bit. They both looked sad.

Mr Pearson started by telling Ginger that they were just following up their investigation about a serious case of cyber-bullying and that whilst her name HAD been mentioned, they just needed her to clear her name so that they could focus on the real culprits.

"Could I have a moment alone with Ginger, please, Jim?" asked Mrs Masterson, fluttering her eyelashes a little but steely eyed, all the same. Had Ginger thought that swearing was an acceptable use of language she might have used a bad word just then.

Alone in the room, Ginger could hear the buzz of the fluorescent strip lights and children outside. She tried to savour the sounds as though they were the last she would ever hear. *Oh, innocent youth, how you laugh and frolic with such abandon in the weak spring sunlight! How I will miss you! Oh glaring electric light strip! How you have lit-up my life with your intrusive yet helpful glare! How I will miss you!*

"You've had a hard time lately, haven't you Ginger?"

Not getting any comprehendible response, she continued.

"I know that you've had stuff going on at home. Your Mum called in to see me a while ago. Asked me to keep an eye on you."

*Stupid Mum! Stupid Mum!*

"I also know that you've had a few problems in school. I know that you've been bullied yourself." She put down the pen she was fiddling with and waited for Ginger to respond.

It took about three minutes for Ginger to make up her mind about what to do next. She twisted her favourite leopard print scarf in knots whilst weighing up the pros and cons of spilling the beans.

It must have been a reflex mechanism but her mind briefly wandered to *whether she could persuade Mum to buy her some lemon Converse for the spring* and from nowhere, *whether or not frogs had noses*. She also knew that that was called *procrastination.*

"Mrs Masterson, I am going to tell you a story about a girl so cruelly cursed with her hair, her giraffe legs and unsuitable parents that she once wandered from the path of good decisions…"

# April

### _The Mystery of the Stolen Pom-Pom: A Bush Valley Cheerleader Mystery_

#### _Reviewed by Ginger Mclean_

_Firstly, I must make it clear that the only reason I read this great novel was because there was nothing else left on the book-trolley and might I add, it pains me that teachers do not get as cross as I do that good books are festering in other people's school bags, unread and wasted._

_That said, I approached reading this novel with my usual enthusiasm. Sadly, I wanted to see the Bush Valley Cheerleading Squad come down with a nasty case of food poisoning from the very start._

_I have experienced some truly troubling events since beginning my journey through high school and none of them involved pom-poms. If indeed, I were to come across a real pom-pom catastrophe, I would hope it involved a cheerleader choking upon one as she approached the final thrilling fall from the human pyramid._

_I would recommend this book to people who are far less intelligent than me and, probably, only to those who have iPhones with pink koala cases._

The series of events that followed the meeting with Mrs Masterson and Mr Pearson at the end of March were all unpleasant.

Firstly, the drama geeks had stopped talking to her. They pretended to be trees or statues when she passed them in the refectory. Popularity was fragile, she had learnt. Only Tom spoke to her but even he was a bit miffed that she had hung up on him.

Other school mates looked at her differently. Mostly as though she was the freak they had always suspected her to be. From this she learnt that the only way she could feel normal was to stay at home with various illnesses ranging from a painful verruca to probably tuberculosis.

Milo stopped trying to annoy her and was entirely business-like when they had to do a paired task. She couldn't be sure, but she thought that he marked her down in peer assessments. In Maths, she saw that he looked pleased to be teamed up with Stephanie instead of her.

Frances, more than ever, looked at her with a look of surprise and disappointment. Her eyebrows were constantly raised in a way that said 'how could you?'

Furthermore, Stephanie Sykes, cleared of Chihuahua kissing, worked the crowds like Taylor Swift. Her popularity was more sickeningly grand than ever. Worse, not only was she followed around by her Barbie-clones but now also a group of the more, erm, challenged members of Year 7 who hailed her a hero for coping with cyber-bullying. They could be heard to talk about how great it was to know that even popular girls can be bullied and wasn't her hair so incredibly shiny? Ginger had been reassured by Mrs Masterson that Stephanie would suffer for bullying, but she kept that quiet from her followers. Ginger might have told them herself but *nobody* wanted to know her side of the story. It was as if Stephanie was purely the victim of abuse, no more guilty than a vulnerable puppy. Or Chihuahua.

But few of these events were as bad as the sense that she had let herself down. It wasn't that she felt so bad about upsetting Beach Barbie, but more that she'd sunk to her level.

Now, she felt as though she was pretty much on her own all of the time. Break times felt like they went on forever so she found excuses to rehearse her cello or finish art projects that didn't exist. She practically ran home from school and spent the rest of the evening redrafting homework and eating crisps. Occasionally she would go round to Tom's and they would watch soaps together but her heart wasn't in it and neither was his. One night he told her to pull herself together. He told her lots of other things she needed to change about herself too. None of it was to do with her hair and all of it was to do with how good a friend she was and how stuck up she could be.

"You're not the only one with problems. Get over yourself!" he said and went back to the magazine he was reading.

Inevitably, Mum and Dad were eventually called into school and followed Quentin's parents into a meeting with Mr Pearson and Mrs Masterson.

Ginger hadn't warned them beforehand what they were going in to discuss. Something in her couldn't shape the words to explain it. Ginger knew that if she began to talk about what she had done she might also begin to talk about what was wrong in her life and that would take longer. So instead she'd mumbled something about how it was probably something to do with her not owning an iPhone.

"Thank you for coming, Mr and Mrs Mclean..."

"Oh, please, Mr Pearson..." piped up Mum. "I'm not using that name at the moment. It's Matthews."

Dad shot her a tired look and both of them looked at the floor with embarrassment.

"There's been a few problems recently. Ginger has got mixed up in a few incidents of bullying." Sensing the stress rising in the room at his revelation he pointed out quickly that in many cases Ginger had been the victim and in others, well... she had not been the victim.

As he explained some of the events of the last couple of months, Ginger clung on to her chair and wondered how Mum and Dad were going to make all of this much worse than it already was.

She needn't have wondered too hard.

"This is exactly the kind of situation that occurs when fathers leave their impressionable and vulnerable off-spring because they are having a mid-life crisis!" screamed Mum, wringing her hands in frustration.

"Oh, of course! Why am I not surprised that this has happened? The girl has no decent role-model in her life! She must get her terrible temper, lying skills and victimisation complex from her mother!" Dad turned to Mr Pearson. "See what I have had to put up with?"

Mr Pearson shot her Dad a sympathetic look and changed the subject.

"In light of all of this mess I wonder if perhaps, erm, Stephanie and Ginger need to get together for a pow-wow. Nothing clears the air like a good chin-wag."

*Pow-wow? Chin-wag?* Ginger shivered.

"Oh yes," added Mum, reluctantly agreeing with Dad, but keen to show that they could work as a team.

"Right-oh," said Mr Pearson. "I think that rather than give out any specific punishments, this should be the course of action." He adjusted his tie smugly, proud that the potentially tricky meeting had gone so well and so swiftly. "I'll leave it to Mrs M to sort out the practicalities." He got up to leave and Mrs Masterson twisted uncomfortably in her chair and shot him daggers as he swept away.

The teacher then looked at Ginger carefully; she was the first adult to do so during the meeting and it was not a good feeling. Adults were so much better when they were talking about their stupid adult world and leaving kids to get on with running it.

"So, we could get you girls together today to talk it through. Both of you get to say how the bullying made you feel. Both of you get to say how things can be resolved…We could do it in the library after school."

Mum was clearly keen to make this work and Dad looked as if he were just glad that there was a plan. A plan that was brilliant because it didn't involve him and he could go for a run or a pint to clear his head.

Then Mum piped up again: "That is a good idea but perhaps I have a better one. I know Stephanie's Mum. Her and Ginger have been right through school together. I'd like to see her and apologise for Ginger's behaviour. So, why don't I give her a call and invite her and Stephanie over for a coffee this week. We can chat about old times and put all this to bed."

A low moan that sounded like a hippo having a splinter removed came from Ginger. "Great idea, Mum. The start of a beautiful friendship! NOT."

"How do you know if you don't give it a try, Ginger?"

Mrs Masterson looked apprehensive. Her eyes communicated to Ginger that she too thought it was unlikely that a beautiful friendship was on the horizon.

"Okay, well why don't you try that this week? Give me a call and tell me how it goes, yes?"

Mum agreed and then changed the subject to how her daughter was doing in her lessons. Clearly Mum hoped that this would close the conversation on a positive note. She was wrong.

"Ginger started wonderfully, as you know. She is a very clever girl and I'm sure you've helped her to be that way. However, she really hasn't made much progress since October. She started well but hasn't really come much further."

This was probably the worst news her parents could have received. Ginger getting good levels at school was as predictable as the story lines in *Hannah Montana*.

"How about in IT lessons? Does her lack of iPhone prevent her from doing well?"

"I wouldn't have thought so. In fact, I doubt that having an iPhone is a good thing for any of us!" she laughed, like a traitor giving up trade secrets from Apple to Microsoft.

"Indeed," agreed Mum and Dad in unison, as though they had spent their lives in constant agreement.

It took very little time to get ready for the tea-party from hell and Ginger didn't care in the slightest about how it went, so long as it got Mum off her back and kept Mrs Masterson happy. She was finishing off another book review. This time she was happy to do it. She'd read *The Boy in the Striped Pyjamas* three weeks before she knew she'd be asked to do it. Mum hadn't let her have a break from homework since she had got home from school and everything else was completed. If anything, getting back into doing homework and generally being a boffin helped Ginger to cope with things. This week she had taken to making up her own homework again. Just for fun.

She heard the doorbell go and took a peak from the bathroom window to see what fresh hell awaited her. It was indeed gruesome. Mother and daughter in nearly matching leggings and top-knot hair styles. Ginger tried to remember what Mum had been wearing when she'd got home from school but couldn't. Whatever monstrosity it was, it was unlikely to match her own outfit: a jersey sweater with a large 'R' printed on it (R for rebel, she hoped) and boyfriend jeans (that were *supposed* to be short, which made a nice change).

Nearly causing her to fall out through the window, Adam grabbed her from behind and said lots of unsympathetic things before changing tact and giving her a pat on the back.

Alex had stayed on the phone long enough the night before to hear the whole sorry story and was cross that she hadn't been able to help sooner. "Why didn't you tell me this was going on, you doofus?"

"It is hard to explain. I kind of blanked out the stuff I didn't want to think or talk about. I didn't want to cause a fuss or draw attention. Whenever I talk to Mum all she pays attention to is my teeth. I could tell her I was joining a troop of roller-skating nuns and she would only be thinking about how much an orthodontist might cost."

"Yeah, I know what you mean. Do you remember when I got mine and she would only let me eat soup for two years? The woman is obsessed with our dental health."

"What should I do, Alex?"

"Just ride out the storm. Smile sweetly at Mrs Sykes. Do your homework and try hard for Mum. Keep your head down..." Alex paused and coughed down the phone so loudly that Ginger had to remove the handset from her ear. "I do think you should get it sorted out with Franny though. She's worth hanging onto. She's good for you."

Ginger knew that would be a bigger battle. There could be no faking it with Frances. She had let down her best friend by not listening to her or talking to her about what was going on in Chateau Mclean. She had only thought of herself all year and was lucky that even Tom had stuck with her. It was also no surprise that Frances had gone and found a new friendship group. What choice had she had with a best friend like Ginger?

Thinking about this made Ginger feel like crawling into bed and never coming out; every part of her body was hurting and trembling – but she had to pull herself together. She'd have to leave her blubbering for later, knowing that she would be loudly trumpeting herself to sleep that night, and disguising the nose-blowing with the soundtrack to *High School Musical* or perhaps something with out of tune guitars from Adam's iPod.

Now, in the kitchen, Mrs Sykes, or Carol (as Mum called her) was leaning into the breakfast bar and saying that she remembered how terrible it was when she was at school when girls had fallen out. Luckily, she told Ginger's Mum, she was pretty and popular but it must have been awful for the more studious and mousey types. She said this whilst looking sympathetically at Mum.

It was clear who would have been who had they gone to school together.

As Ginger walked in, Carol looked her up and down with the same sympathetic eyes. "Well, Ginger! How you've grown. You'll be needing to get a bra in the next few years!"

It was fairly obvious that whilst Stephanie nodded in agreement with her mother's observations, she subtly adjusted her own amply filled bra-cup.

They retreated to the lounge where Carol sipped the tea

that she had brought herself – something with berries in it that had apparently been regurgitated by Brazilian vampire bats and was good for the skin – whilst Ginger, Stephanie and her Mum sipped ordinary tea.

Carol told them about how Martin, Steph's Dad, had just bought three new properties in town and was renting them out to poor immigrants and making a killing. She was very proud of this. Consequently, Stephanie might go to private school next year unless they bought another Range Rover Vogue. They couldn't decide which was more important.

Carol then asked where Mr Mclean was; she wasn't sure of his first name, she said. What Ginger was sure she *was* sure of was that Mr and Mrs Mclean had split last year.

"Well, Carol, I'm sorry to say that we have separated. I'm more likely to be spending my hard earned wages on a lawyer than a 4X4."

"Oh, that's sad!" replied Carol, reproducing many of the same acting devices that her daughter had employed over the last couple of weeks: eyebrows raised like lab-bunnies, mouths pulled into tiny dog-bottom like pouts...

The conversation then moved to how the girls were doing at Atherton. Apparently Stephanie was making great grades in all her subjects and her teachers were delighted with her. Ginger nearly scoffed but held it in like a burp. Stephanie was not doing great. She spent all her time in lessons being told off for gossiping with her pouting mates about who definitely fancied her and who probably fancied her and whether or not her hair parting looked best in the centre or at the side. Then there were the constant 'selfies':

photographs taken of themselves pulling faces that managed to make them both look cute and goofy at the same time.

Perhaps the world of technology WAS too much for Ginger. She made a plan to do some research into living in the countryside with wolves although she would have to use books in a library to do it rather than Google, she decided.

Mum tried to look interested but was clearly impatient that they get down to business.

"So, how can we resolve the little problems you two have been having?" she said when there was a polite gap in the Stephanie appreciation chatter.

Little?

Ginger was not about to be the first to speak.

Stephanie, however, was quite eager.

"Well, Mrs Mclean, or might I call you Annabel...?"

"Urm, yes of course, dear." Yet Mum did not look happy. She clearly didn't think that children and parents were meant to be friends. She had made that clear for around the last twelve years of Ginger's life. Ginger was quietly pleased about this one constant in their family dynamic. She certainly didn't want to have one of those mothers who thought that they were her daughter's best friend! Embarrassing!

"Annabel, I want to say that I'm sorry if Ginger thinks I did something to hurt her. I really didn't mean to do wrong, but I have. And that makes me feel terrible." Cue tears and tissue. "I for one would be more than happy to forgive

Ginger if only she will forgive me for anything that I may have done wrong, though most of it was actually that cow Lydia who I will not be inviting to my spa party next week."

Her Mum looked at Ginger with something like the same face she used when she had just bought a new outfit and modelled it for her children to gauge their opinion. Blind hope and exhaustion.

Ginger was forced to speak but her usually extensive vocabulary and way with words failed her miserably. There was no point in wasting words on this.

"Uh-uh. Okay. I forgive you."

"Eh, erm, Ginger?" pleaded her Mum, using her hands to try to magic more words from her daughter's mouth.

"Yeah, okay, I'm sorry too."

A small clap came from Carol and even Ginger's Mum looked relieved.

"Oh, how wonderful. This has been such a nice visit. I would suggest that Ginger come to Stephanie's spa party next month but I wonder if she's really into that kind of thing. Perhaps next year, when we have another pony party? You do like ponies, don't you?"

Ginger didn't bother to answer but just looked at her watch and mumbled something about her homework not doing itself. Mum hurriedly mentioned getting the dinner on before Adam came down and started eating the furniture.

If there was one skill in which the Mcleans were all equals, it was not dragging out a conversation about emotions.

When Carol and Stephanie had gone, they'd finished dinner and Ginger told her Mum that she was popping over to see Frances. Mum raised her eyebrows but didn't argue.

Ginger too had secret weapons: a couple of jam-jars and a sharp pair of garden scissors. It was rose-perfume o'clock and nobody would stop her.

She knocked on the door. This would be the biggest battle of her life and, probably, the most important.

Frances arrived at the door in fluffy slippers that were shaped like Labradors. She had been wearing them since they were given to her for Christmas three years ago and must have been too small for her.

Ginger was used to Franny wearing an expression of confusion but this one was perhaps the most bewildered she had ever seen.

"What… what are you doing here?"

"I erm, brought something." With shaking hands, Ginger produced the jam-jars from behind her back.

"But I don't understand…"

Nervously, Ginger coughed and set about her best impression of Frances' grandfather, all those years ago: "Now, you young ladies, if I ever catch you near my rose beds again I'll 'ave your guts for garters!"

She felt a bit stupid afterwards because Frances' expression had barely moved. It was like it was the wind had changed and stuck it permanently in astonishment.

Eventually, Frances spoke.

"Look Ginger, that was a long time ago. Things have

changed. I don't want to be in your shadow all the time. It turns out that I'm pretty cool in my own right and to be honest, I'm better at high school than you are."

"Yes. I know. You're a LOT better at high school than me. But then so are Brittany and Hermione."

"You were not a good friend to me."

Ginger dropped her eyes to the doorstep and thought that Frances was quite right. She hadn't been a good friend for a long time.

"I know. But I'm sorry. I know what a loser I've been."

"You're not a loser," admitted Frances. "But you do need to learn a few things about friendship."

Frances began to cry.

"You just didn't care about my stuff."

Ginger had never felt so awful in her life. She could have spray painted rude words about Stephanie across the sports hall windows and she couldn't have felt this guilty. She had known this would be hard but couldn't have imagined that it would be this rough.

"I did care. I just didn't know I cared because I was too wrapped up in my own problems. It never occurred to me that you needed me. I never meant to hurt you."

"I could have really helped when your Mum and Dad broke up. I wanted to help."

Frances wiped her tears away and brushed herself down.

"Look, you've upset Butch and Billy now!"

Ginger look at Frances in puzzlement for a moment before she realised that Frances was making a joke. Of course! Butch and Billy were her Labrador slippers.

"Tell them that I've missed them," insisted Ginger, giggling as her friend tried to keep a straight face.

"Granddad won't let us use his roses, you know. We might have to make do with Mum's pansies. Some of them are out."

"I heard that!" came a voice from inside the house and the two girls laughed a little less uncomfortably.

Instead, they sat on the mossy wall behind Frances' house. The sun was low in the sky but it was fairly warm for the time of year.

"It's my birthday next week. I'm going to Alton Towers for the day. Mum said I can invite a friend."

Ginger's ears perked up. Things were going well.

"I've already asked Rebecca. Do you mind?"

For every year as long as she could remember, they had spent Frances' birthday at a theme park. If it weren't for Frances' family Ginger would never have been on a roller-coaster. Dad didn't seem to believe in taking his children on days out to actual fun places.

"No, I understand," replied Ginger, honestly. "I like Rebecca."

The girls then sat in silence for a few minutes and the months fell away like petals as they each realised how easy a friendship could be if you tried just a little bit to understand each other's point of view.

# May

It had never occurred to Ginger that Milo Costigan lived in a house like a mortal. She always imagined him in a beach shack, surrounded by surf boards or possibly a tree house where he would be dressed every morning by sparrows and blue birds; perhaps even by a wise owl with a deep baritone. As it turned out, he was now living on the estate behind Ginger's own semi-detached house.

It was Bank Holiday weekend and Mum had sent her to the shop for some milk in an attempt to get her outside. It was probably family camping holidays that had ruined the outdoors for Ginger. There was nothing like finding a wasp in your sleeping bag for spoiling your friendship with nature.

To be fair to her mother, the sunshine did feel nice on her shoulders. She had picked out a vest top in an attempt to make the trip worthwhile and hopefully bring back a sporty tan. This, she knew, was unlikely. If she picked anything up on her stroll through the blossomed avenues, it was likely to be four more freckles and some dog poo on her flip-flops. There was a lot of talk about tans at school at the moment. She had noticed that a lot of girls had suspiciously brown-streaked palms and tide-marks around their necks.

Tans were the new bras. Everyone was talking about them.

Even though the shop was only ten minutes' walk, Ginger had taken her birthday rucksack and filled it with SPF50, some spray deodorant (she was never without it these days) and her purse. Perhaps she'd buy some magazines with her pocket money. There was still room for the milk, which she would rather not be seen carrying home.

Frances couldn't come because she had a church thing to go to and Ginger did really believe her today. This was a new era of honesty and her and Frances had slowly but surely made things right again. The previous week they had even drawn the curtains and played 'Princesses get chased by witch' which had resulted in Frances laughing so much that she was sick all over her carpet. Ginger had even asked if she could see the photographs from the trip to Alton Towers. It looked like they'd had a great time. Ginger consoled herself with the fact that the water rides would have played havoc with her hair.

Outside the shop there were some older boys who clearly thought they were in Greece because they had forgotten to wear their shirts. Perhaps their mothers hadn't done the washing that day or perhaps Topman had run out of t-shirts. Who knew? They looked ridiculous. All of them were sharing a cigarette and she guessed that their purpose was to find a fool who was old enough to buy them some cider.

As she got closer she saw that coming out of the shop was Adam. In stark contrast to the other boys, Adam was, as usual, wearing a black un-ironed shirt, a grey knitted sweater with a hole near the neck plus a hoody with a skull on the back. His jeans hung below his hips and were strangely tight where they met his old trainers. She could practically smell those trainers from across the street.

*Nostril memory*, she thought. *Amazing.*

Though she couldn't make out what was being said, she could see that Adam had become engaged in a conversation with the shirt-off crew. *Perhaps they were discussing the crisis in Syria*, wondered Ginger.

Soon she could make out the conversation and was alarmed by how uncomfortable Adam looked.

The smallest of the boys, distinguishable by his runty arms and some reflective sunglasses was saying: "You're weird. Look at how you dress! You look poor. Do you shop in charity shops?" He was pointing and laughing as though Adam were a funny YouTube video.

Ginger felt her temperature rise as she witnessed this. She hated Adam most of the time but he was HER brother and this was not acceptable. It had never occurred to her that Adam could be a victim. She had always been quite comfortable that she was his victim, but here he was in her accustomed (if slightly more masculine) role - the geek with sweaty feet and about five power chords to his name.

Adam was now pressed up against the shop front, his head oddly close to a large cut-out of Harry Styles behind the glass which made it look as though Harry was holding him so that the boys could give him a beating. Adam towered above the other boy but didn't seem to be giving as good as he got.

Ginger quickened her pace, unsure of what she would say but sure she needed to intervene. She didn't see the 4x4 Range Rover coming towards her but did hear someone shouting to warn her. Ginger performed a side-step which would have impressed her dance teacher and realised that the voice had come from none other than Milo Costigan. Inadvertently, they had both arrived at the scene in a pincer movement and were both now just behind the crowd of boys and her brother.

It was not the time or the place to let her mind wander but Ginger couldn't help noticing how great Milo looked in the spring sun. Her heart lurched a little bit when she thought of how good he was at the really tricky algebra they had been learning recently. And at how she felt when she heard him play in orchestra. Why couldn't she just be cool around him? What was wrong with her?

All thoughts of romance were banished when she heard a strange yelp.

The not very manly noises were coming from Adam. Ginger wasn't sure but thought she heard him say that he wanted his Mum.

"What are you doing here?" she asked Milo.

"Getting some milk for my Mum," he replied, pushing his long fringe out of his eyes.

Milo got milk for his Mum?

"Why are you here though, at this shop?"

"Durh, because I live on Cyprus Street."

They eyed each other suspiciously for a moment before Ginger remembered what was going on and inspected the violent scene in front of her. It looked as though Adam was about to get a wedgie and from experience of being the youngest sibling, she knew that she had to do something.

She attempted to walk confidently into the throng of

boys, pushing the weakest looking in the sunglasses to get past him.

"Excuse me!" she shouted in her best grown-up voice. She thought it sounded a bit like Claudia Winkleman's and felt her self-esteem growing. She was also assisted by the fact that she was as tall as the tallest boy in the group. At least she wasn't wasting good height genes!

"Who are you?" asked a boy with a complex series of razor lines across the side of his head. *Stylish*, she thought, *if you're in prison.*

"It doesn't matter what my name is..." she began, hardly wanting to draw them into further discussion around her stupid name.

Stupid parents! Dave and Annabel could manage to make any situation worse!

"Ginger!" called Adam and Milo at once. Milo was right behind her, she noticed. Many years of embarrassment and goose-bumps had taught her to sense his proximity.

"Ginger! Ha!" echoed the big boys.

This wasn't helping, she thought.

"Look, there is no point in beating my brother up because he hasn't got any money. I know this because he asked Mum for some this morning and she flat refused. Also, he has a can of some awful caffeine drink in his pocket and I surmise that he has just purchased that from the shopkeeper with any remaining change he had. I can confidently say that he has no money."

Adam was now crying, whilst simultaneously miming a strangle, which she couldn't be sure wasn't for her.

"We don't want his money. We've got our own," the boy who was holding Adam against the window turned to say to her. "This is just for fun." With this, the boy reached around the back of Adam and wrenched his underpants upwards.

The sound that came from Adam was almost so high in pitch that only woodland creatures could have heard it. But not quite.

Then, just as the boy dropped Adam and pulled his foot back as if to kick Adam, Ginger, leapt up onto the assailant's back and held on to his hair. This didn't stop the kick and Adam was now holding onto his right shin as if he were a Premiership footballer.

Behind her, she felt the presence of the other boys who were moving in to pull her off.

She could smell the sickly smell of alcohol on their breath like a chemical weapon designed to knock you out at ten paces. They were laughing as they tried to get her off and so busy that they didn't see Milo throw the contents of a bottle of water over their heads from behind. This caused them to turn their attention to him and explain things like "Oy!" and "Nobody messes with my hair."

The distraction allowed Ginger to try out a new tactic and she dropped down and began to hit the boy who was holding Adam with her bag. The SPF was a large family sized bottle that nobody had used yet. It packed a punch.

Adam was lying on the floor next to some broken glass, Milo was running in circles being chased by the rest of the boys and Ginger was beating Adam's attacker with her bag when the police arrived.

The nee-naws hadn't got Ginger's attention because in her entire life, nee-naws had always been someone else's problem.

She found herself being lifted from the waist by a strangely small looking officer who struggled to handle her height and sudden super-human strength.

"Calm it down, young lady!" He shouted in her ear and eventually got enough of a grip to haul her backwards away from the cowering body of Adam's attacker.

When she realised that she was a few metres away and could focus on the scene, Ginger's heart rate began to calm. *Flipping stupid Adam,* she thought to herself. *Why couldn't he wear clean clothes and just be like a normal person who didn't get himself beaten up outside the Premier Stores on pleasant spring days?*

Another officer had retrieved her flip-flops and was applying them to her feet as he said, "We'll need you to come down to the station with us now, love." Ginger tried to get her phone out of her bag. She would have to call for help. Alex was her only hope!

However, the policeman gently took the bag off her before she could grope for it anymore.

"Don't worry, we'll call your parents."

The taste of sickness flowed up from some deep place in Ginger's stomach and within moments, she found herself in a police car with Milo and Adam and two lady police officers, unsure of how she got there.

"It is a good thing that Mrs Sykes and her daughter saw the whole thing, sir. Said they were driving back from the nail salon when they nearly hit an object on the main road. They called us because they thought that some young men were in danger of getting GBH from a young lady with untameable hair."

Dad looked at Ginger who had her head down on the desk and looked somewhat like Cousin It from the Addam's family.

"I am so sorry," began Dad. "Is the young man okay?"

"He's fine. Very bruised but no worse than your son. They'll both be fine."

Dad looked relieved but then as he turned to Mum, he was clearly angry.

"How could this have happened? What has happened to Ginger? First she's cyber-bullying and now she's beating up teenage boys in the street? What kind of mother are you?"

"What about those thugs, Dave? They were the problem not our kids!"

Just as Mum was about to go on when the PC interrupted to tell them what he thought had actually happened.

"The young man, Milo, was very helpful. He explained what occurred. I don't think you should be too hard on your daughter. No charges will be pressed."

This did not satisfy Dad, who was clearly convinced that Ginger had become a juvenile delinquent and would probably soon be carted off to a young offender's institution.

"She's twelve, Annabel!" he said to Mum.

In the car park, Ginger found Milo and a lady that looked as though she was his Mum. She also had blonde floppy hair and a nice smile. Whilst Mum and Dad continued to argue, Ginger stood with them and tried to distract everyone from her parents' discussion.

Adam was lurking in the background, nursing his behind and looking really fed-up. Ginger felt a pang of love for her stupid brother and resolved to let him have the DVDs back that she'd hidden from him months ago when he was being a pain. She knew that it had been him who was sneaking into her room and rearranging her pencils so that she thought she was going crazy for a while. She would forgive him for that. He really needed all the victories he could get these days.

It was peculiar feeling but suddenly she didn't feel so nervous being near Milo. Yes, she wished she had a hair bobble, but that was nothing new. She could that he was just a boy, with a Mum and a house on Cyprus Street.

"You were pretty cool today, you know."

"Thanks," she said, meaning it.

"What a day. Look, this is my Mum."

Milo's Mum reached out a hand and Ginger noticed that it was very thin and covered in lines. Looking at her face she could see a familiar look, one like her own Mum's: a bit tired and sad.

"I'm Sarah. Pleased to meet you. I hear you were quite heroic today."

Sarah! Even her name sounded calm and full of

normality.

"Or a delinquent. Your point of view depends on whether you are a member of my family or not."

"Ha-ha, well I'm sure it'll all work out. Is your brother okay?"

"Yes, he's fine. I mean he's a dork, but we can't do anything about that."

They all laughed and then Ginger had to go and get into her Mum's hatchback whilst Dad screeched off in the Volvo with some loud folk music blaring from the windows.

# June

*Diary of a Delinquent: Cell Life*

*By Ginger Mclean*

*Paragraph 1:*

*A rodent scuttles somewhere in a corner. The girl doesn't even lift her head. She used to shout out but stopped when she realised that no one was listening. She tries to busy her mind with homework, but it does little to relieve the numbness. Outside the cell, she can hear life. None of it matters to her anymore. Nobody would remember her name. Not even if it were followed by 'You remember, the one who viciously attacked those innocent boys outside the Premier Stores'.*

Mum was replacing the hand-set in its cradle and humming something cheerful to herself when Ginger arrived home from school. This didn't make Ginger feel confident. Mum in an 'I'm-so-pleased-with-myself' mood usually meant trouble.

Her day at school had gone relatively well. Perhaps she was finally settling into high school life and all her hopes and dreams would be fulfilled. Probably, she would be very popular soon and her hair would settle down.

Milo was now almost a friend.

Frances was back on the team.

A few times, Ginger, Milo and Frances had walked home from orchestra practice together. Once, they had even had detour to the chippy and shared chips and curry sauce.

Much of why school had become bearable was because the news of her deeds at the shop had spread like head-lice amongst the student body of Atherton Academy. This was entirely traceable to Stephanie Sykes who had spread the rumours that she had been held at gun-point and that Ginger was a violent psychopath.

Being known as a psychopath was not so bad. Everyone left you alone and nobody wanted to ask you any details.

Also, school was much better than home recently.

Milo obviously knew the truth and between them there was a new un-spoken history of crime-fighting and respect. By putting their minds together they could not only battle with the common criminal mind but also solve any mathematical problem placed in their path. They worked together wherever possible in lessons and were a force to be reckoned with. Ginger was finally making progress again.

Her nerves had stopped bothering her too. No longer did her palms sweat or did she check for bogies when he was within ear-shot. Sometimes, she even let it slide when his planner overlapped her side of the desk.

This relative peace was in contrast to the atmosphere in the Mclean home.

Adam hadn't spoken to her since the incident. He went about his usual strange business of mooning around over girls, playing squash and breaking things but, mostly, he was out of the house. She seriously hoped that he was staying out of trouble and that she wouldn't have to rescue him again. Being heroic was exhausting.

Mum, unfortunately, was on some kind of parenting and talking overdrive. Nothing slipped past her anymore. It was like being in a Petri-dish in a science lab.

Dr Mclean (Mum), was carefully experimenting with different approaches to turning Ginger's life around.

She had taken the heavy-handed approach to begin with. Ginger had been grounded (which seemed fairly pointless as Ginger was hardly likely to miss going out to night-clubs or hanging around on street corners). This had also involved her Mum sticking her head into her bedroom every twenty-seven seconds to check she wasn't taking drugs or designing bombs for terrorist organisations.

The following week, Mum had played her guilt card. This had more impact: "How could you do this to us, Ginger?"... "Didn't I give you enough attention when you were little?"... "Is it because I let you eat chicken nuggets when you wouldn't eat anything else?"... "I have tried so hard!"... "I am a terrible mother!"

Ginger had spent a week listening to her mother's wails and snorts and saying things like: "It isn't your fault!"... "Nobody is to blame."... "I'm so sorry!"... "Perhaps if you'd let me have more chicken nuggets."

The previous weekend, Alex had returned from university and announced that they had all gone mad in her absence and that she would not be leaving to complete her final year if they didn't sort themselves out. This had brought about some change in Mum.

This week, the tears had dried up and now her Mum was singing Michael Bublé and wrapping a present in pastel pink tissue paper.

"Ah, there you are. You are quite late but I think there's time."

"It's Friday night. I do orchestra. We've got to be ready for Sports Day and we're awful. I've suggested to Mr Arnold that he really should rethink his if-you-want-to-play-you-will attitude. We sound like a bunch of amateurs." Ginger slumped at the breakfast bar and began to make a tower out of the vegetables that were waiting to be prepared for dinner.

"Well, anyway, I've decided that you need a bit of space..."

"Oh yes, does this mean...," started Ginger, hoping that this meant that Mum and Adam were both going out and that her and Alex would have the house to themselves for the weekend.

No such luck, as her Mum continued.

"I've just got off the phone with Carol. You are going to experience the wonders of spa-therapy and making friends with people who do not encourage you to break the law. Stephanie and Carol are looking forward to it. The party starts at 6.30. You better pack your tooth brush and a smile."

The mushroom tower crashed down around her.

Mum, however, was so delighted with herself that, had she been in a panto, she would have slapped her thigh at this point.

It wasn't a particularly hot June day but Ginger had to loosen her collar. A creeping sweat enveloped her body and she began to feel light headed and as though a thousand wasps were having a slumber party in her tummy. She steadied herself on the worktop to stop herself falling.

Seriously? She thought, pulling herself together. Was this worse than finding out your parents were getting divorced, hearing that you wet the bed from a Year 10 or that your favourite flavour of lip-balm had been discontinued?

"YOU have GOT to be KIDDING!"

"Ah, I thought you might say that," replied Mum, fully prepared for such a response. "It will be great. Look, I've bought you some new pyjamas especially. Here."

A set of pyjamas tumbled onto the kitchen top. The t-shirt was cropped whilst the faces of small tortured kittens glared at her with big eyes from the jersey cotton bottoms, laughing at her pain.

"And look, I got some for Stephanie as a present. They match yours but have puppies instead of cats. Aren't they adorable?"

"It BURNS! It burns!" squealed Ginger at the spectacle of the pyjamas.

"Don't be so silly. Get changed and I'll drop you off in half an hour."

To punctuate the end of the conversation, Mum picked up the phone and dialled a number. When Ginger made to protest further her Mum simply made a 'Shush!' gesture and turned her back.

"Oh, hi, Robin. Look, I have the house to myself tonight so why don't you swing by with some wine?"

On the stairs, Ginger didn't even bother to move out of the way for Alex. She just bumped into her and mumbled before running up to her room and slamming the door. Inevitably, her bedroom door opened just as she was climbing into bed fully dressed with her shoes on.

"What is going on? It's like coming home to a reality TV show. This place! I keep checking for cameras."

Ginger had to confide in someone and Alex was always understanding. She would know what to do!

The clock was ticking but it took much longer than it should have done to explain because Ginger's brain couldn't seem to form any coherent sentence, let alone put the information in an order that made sense:

"Urgh, kittens... spa party, pyjamas with... Hate her... Rather go to a One Direction concert... Her birthday...

Hate face masks… Mum knows that…Puppies…I hate my life! Calling Childline…" she wept into her favourite purple duvet cover, smearing it with snot.

"Ah, I see," Alex said sarcastically. "It all makes perfect sense now…"

"I just can't go. They will make my life hell. Everyone knows I'm allergic to spa-products and kittens! They'll pin me down and wax me until I look like a bald meerkat!"

"Look, just calm down. It might be fun."

Ginger just looked at Alex. Alex had obviously left her brain at university.

"I'm afraid that there's nothing I can do. I've been persuading Mum to let me go to the festival all week and she's finally agreed. I can't risk her changing her mind. I can't get involved in this. You need to have a positive mind-set. If all else fails, you'll have an invaluable insight into the nocturnal habits of the common or garden air-head. Think of yourself as Attenborough, unravelling the mysteries of a tribe. We'll be laughing about it on Sunday."

In an unusual act of violence directed at her preferred sibling, Ginger knocked Alex clean off the bed with one swoop of a pillow.

"Blimey, perhaps Mum has a point. You are a psychopath!" said Alex laughing and pulling herself together. "See you soon, Bear Grylls."

Ginger slammed the car door and the hatchback rocked. Mum still looked like the Cheshire Cat as she waved and blew a kiss. Ginger threw one back thinking that that would the last kiss her Mum would ever get from her. Or at least until she agreed to buy Ginger a more expensive handbag. Possibly one from the Mulberry shop in the Victorian Quarter.

Carol Sykes was in the garden, sipping a drink that was festooned with an umbrella and a slice of pineapple. *At least Mum didn't do anything quite that embarrassing*, thought Ginger.

Inside, there was a strange smell in the air; it was similar to what Dad once used to make the car smell better after Adam had been sick in it when he got drunk at the Youth Club and the Youth Leader had angrily demanded that he be picked up.

There was no point in hanging back. The only way to deal with this was to push on for Queen and Country (were Ginger to care about the Queen which she though that she probably didn't). Ginger had long ago decided that Royalty was probably a bit of a waste of time. It wasn't as if the Queen actually could behead anyone or do anything very interesting. She was just an old lady with a dog. She probably watched a lot of *Countdown* like Grandma used to do.

The sound of a Rhianna track was coming from an upstairs room and so she followed it, tracing her fingers along the tufty wallpaper all the way. The pattern reminded her of a labyrinth. She hoped that it would be at this moment that she would discover that she was actually an underworld princess. She would be swallowed up into it and led away to rule over fawns…

Instead, she reached the top of stairs a mortal and had no choice but to follow the ear-numbing screams of "Umbrella".

Ginger shouldn't have been surprised at what she saw, but still it caught her breath.

Standing in a line, girls were throwing shapes around in what they probably thought was a music video-style dance routine. What struck Ginger first was how only Stephanie knew the moves and that the others were trying to follow her with what can only be described as the talent of dancing dogs on *Britain's Got Talent*. Stephanie herself was pumping her arms around like some kind of deranged chimpanzee whilst pouting at every chance she got in the mirror. The entire scene was hilarious.

From a Disney-Princess style four poster bed, Frances was watching intently and stuffing popcorn in her mouth. Ginger thought that she was doing this hungrily so as to disguise how much she wanted to laugh. Laughter was not the response that Stephanie was looking for and finally noticing Ginger in the door-way, she turned off the music and put her hand on her hip in an exaggerated way.

Ginger was just waving over at Frances when the music came to an abrupt stop.

"WHAT, are YOU doing here?" screamed Stephanie, moving so close to Ginger that the make-up cluster-bomb that had gone off on her face was clearly visible. "And WHAT is funny?"

It was now apparent that Stephanie's Mum hadn't mentioned that Ginger would be attending the spa party.

Ginger wondered if this was because she was drunk when she'd agreed to it. She remembered the one time she had seen her own mother after a couple of cocktails and there were plenty of waiters in TGI Friday's who would remember that night too.

"Well, it looks like your Mum was too inebriated to tell you. I am hardly surprised that you turned out like this."

"Like WHAT?" spat Stephanie, delivering a spray of saliva onto Ginger's sweater.

"Urgghhhh," agreed all the girls, including Lydia, who looked a little embarrassed for her friend.

"Just like WRONG, on e-v-e-r-y level."

Suddenly Frances was between them and doing her best to hold them off each other. Stephanie had now turned into Scrappy-Doo, trying desperately to smack Ginger with her left hook whilst Ginger was simply leaning in, using her extreme height to intimidate Stephanie.

Suddenly, all the girls stopped shouting as loud footsteps and some swear words came from the stairs. In an astounding moment of union, all fell into complete silence, waiting to find out who was going to appear at the door next.

Luckily a loud burp on the landing announced that it was only Carol, seemingly making her way to bed and knocking off ornaments and pictures on the way.

"Is your Mum really drunk, Steph?" whispered Ginger.

Stephanie looked at the floor and dropped her hands from the 'let-me-at-her' position they had been clenched in.

"Yeah, probably."

Everyone dusted themselves off and placed themselves in a part of the large bedroom where they wouldn't need to make eye contact with anyone else. Frances had found a particularly fascinating copy of *The Princess Diaries* to flick through; Lydia was exploring her toe-nails.

Stephanie and Ginger sank to the floor and remained silent for about ten minutes.

"You know, parents are all bonkers," Stephanie finally admitted. She wiped a tear away and rubbed a finger under each eye to check for smeared eye-liner.

"God, tell me about it. At least your Mum and Dad are together. Mine only speak through their solicitors now. Losers."

"That is sad but at least you don't have to listen to them fight all the time. Or listen to your Mum getting drunk and singing on the Karaoke machine until four o'clock in the morning."

"Karaoke machine?" Ginger managed.

"Oh yes. She has all these tracks she likes to sing to by sad old country singers. She gets drunker and drunker and louder and louder. We're lucky tonight that she went to bed. THAT would have been TOTALLY humiliating!"

Stephanie and Ginger looked at each other and both laughed in spite of themselves.

"I liked your dance routine," lied Ginger, trying to lessen the pain that Stephanie was obviously feeling, despite her weak smiles.

"No you didn't. But if you like, I can show you how to do it."

"Erm, okay then!" agreed Ginger, thinking that perhaps she had indeed finally had her actual life hijacked by the Disney Channel.

Stephanie went back to her iPod dock and fiddled around for a moment before settling on something by Robin Thicke. *OMG*, thought Ginger, scolding herself for thinking in text speak.

"MEGA LOLZ!" shouted Frances from the bed before joining them. Soon, the room was full of 12-year-old girls attempting to copy Stephanie, pouting and occasionally, falling over.

Looking in the bathroom mirror, Ginger wondered if she was going into anaphylactic shock. Trying to build the fragile bond, she had agreed to have: a cleansing facemask (because she had big pores and blackheads, apparently); her cuticles removed (they were a bit 'maths teacher' she'd been told, not unkindly); a pedicure that involved soaking her feet in something that she thought smelt like the essence of boiled Bratz dolls; every nail on her body painted a coral orange and adorned with a symbol that reminded her of the *X-Factor* logo but in sparkles; her hair plaited in two different directions, undone, straightened, undone, washed, blow-dried and, finally, bleached at the ends so that she had her very own 'dip-dye'.

It had been exhausting. But all of this had seemed to make Stephanie feel better and stop talking about her crazy Mum.

Ginger had drawn a line at an attempt to pierce her belly

button, which she only knew was on the cards when Stephanie came wielding an old kebab skewer towards her exposed tummy (thanks for the puppy pyjamas, Mum).

She got home at around ten o'clock in the morning, entering the kitchen through the back door. Here she found Adam preparing for his usual Saturday plan of picking his long-suffering girlfriend up and making her go to band-practice with him.

Adam did a double take at the sight of his sister but maintained his decision not to speak to her until both their parents were dead and they'd be forced to discuss their inheritance.

Ignoring him, Ginger poured herself a bowl of Coco Pops and some orange juice.

"G-I-N-G-E-R Mclean! What has happened to your face and hair... and...OH... your nails!" came another voice, unmistakably that of Alex, who was standing at the door wearing very dirty wellies and a rucksack that looked as though it had been through World War I.

"I thought you were at a festival?" enquired Ginger, changing the subject.

"We were, but Alfie's tent got washed away last night in a freak hurricane. I couldn't handle it. It was the WORST night of my life."

"Ah, well, it serves you right for abandoning me. I'll be telling a therapist about how my elder sibling sold me out to a spa party when I'm twenty three and can't adjust to normal adult life."

"Yeah, well, sorry about that. It looks like you got your money's worth."

"I know. But it wasn't so bad. It made Stephanie happy and, as you know, I am all about giving something back to those less fortunate than me."

"Is that the *X-Factor* logo on your big toe?" said Adam, giving up his resolution not to speak to his sister ever again as quickly as you could forget the words 'Matt Cardle'.

"Probably. Who cares? I did it. I'm a better person and learnt something about adults. They are all idiots, not just ours." Ginger put down her orange juice wearily, as if she had just completed a long tour of duty in Iraq.

"I like your hair. I always knew you were a blonde, deep down Ginge," whispered Alex, ignoring Adam and putting her arm around Ginger. Ginger pulled away because Alex smelled of something that had been dragged in by the cat.

"So what's the plan for today? Mind if I tag along with you and Dad later?"

"Oh God. I'd forgotten about that."

"Holy-Club House!" squeaked Adam, in his best Minnie Mouse voice. "You really should take up squash. I never have to see them both on a Friday night."

"Well, it looks like things are staying as they are so we may as well get used to things. And Robin is okay. He gave me a cool old t-shirt he bought at a Rolling Stones gig in the 1970s," said Alex, trying to scrape mud from her finger nails in the kitchen sink.

"You know, Ginger, I've been in this family a lot longer than you and whilst it sucks when your parents split up, it is for the best. When I was little, there were a lot more arguments. It was lonely a lot of the time and I didn't have an awesome older sister to talk to. When you came along, they just started having separate lives so you didn't notice that they hated each other. You just thought that that was how families were. Well, they're not. Not happy ones. I remember wishing that they would split up and try to be happy apart. It was pretty rubbish."

Ginger had never thought about the time before she had been around in the Mclean house. Alex was right; Mum and Dad had always done things on their own or with just her, rarely together. Only the annual family trip to France had seen them all together and thinking about it, every summer they had argued.

Did she want her parents to continue to be together but hating every minute of it? Did she want to be the only reason they shared house? Even at their most annoying, they weren't such bad people. Being apart had meant that her Mum had been happy at times and Dad looked healthier than he ever had.

She did want them to be happy.

When Dad arrived to pick them up, Alex smelled less like a wet field and more like herself.

They got into the car to find that Minnie wasn't in it and guiltily, Ginger felt a sense of relief. They needed to have a proper talk.

"Manage not to get yourself incarcerated recently?" laughed Dad.

"What does incarcerated mean?" Ginger asked

suspiciously.

"It means behind bars," giggled Alex.

"Ah, funny. You two should be a double act."

At Nando's, Ginger found herself ordering the largest portion of chicken on the menu. Spa made you hungry! Who knew?

"Girls, now that you're both here. We need to have a proper talk."

The sisters exchanged looks of mutual support and that special sense that sisters have of forever-ness. Whatever he said, they could handle it together.

"Me and your Mum… well, we won't be getting back together. She's happy with Robin. I'm happy too. I know it isn't how you wanted things to go but there it is."

Dad went back to his chicken for a moment, looking into his food like it held the answers.

"You know, it will be okay," he looked so sad. "We're going to be divorced soon. I'm going to buy a house with Sonia."

Ginger chewed on an olive and considered what he was saying. Yes she loved both her parents, even when they were embarrassing and wearing their camping clothes, but she did want to see them having better lives. Perhaps they would even pay more attention to her. Tom was always saying how great it was to have divorced parents because he got twice as many presents at Christmas and double pocket-money. That could be a lot of Topshop vouchers.

"I think we knew that, Dad," said Alex finally. "I remember what it was like when you were both arguing all the time. It was miserable."

"I'm sorry," said Dad. "But it is all going to be fine."

Ginger thought back over the year and wondered if it had been the worst one anyone had ever had. But if there was one thing that she had learnt, it was that everyone has their own problems and that, for once, she was quite normal.

It was another night that month when Ginger was given a night off homework and allowed to have Frances over for dinner.

The two girls lay top-to-toe on Ginger's purple duvet, trying to catch Maltesers in their mouths, waiting for the fiveminute dinner warning.

"I love that you got arrested."

"That was ages ago. Now I'm considering how to hack into the American CIA website and bring down the West."

"You're nuts, you know. I hardly ever know what you are talking about."

"No, you're not alone."

Frances caught a chocolate and leaned over for a high-five. Ginger left her hanging, pretending to be annoyed but then met her friend's hand with a slap.

"Dad and Mum aren't getting back together. Dad is serious about Minnie. They are all so weird."

"Does that mean that you'll be moving in with him and getting a new Mum? Sometimes I'd like a new Mum. It is ridiculous that I have to do so many chores."

"No you don't. And no I won't. It just means that I've got to get used to new things. MORE new things."

"Yeah, this year has been a strange one. For one thing, I never thought a boy would like me...."

"What?" Ginger sat up straight. "WHO?"

"Don't sound so surprise. If you hadn't noticed, I'm looking pretty cute these days!"

"I have noticed! You are looking really great."

"Do you think we're too young to bother about boys? I mean, I like him but it is so rubbish when you see Year 7 and 8s acting like they're getting married. Stephanie once said that she was getting engaged to that boy in Florida. As if!"

"Totally lame, I agree. I think it is nice to have boys as friends though. Look at Tom. He's definitely my second best friend and one of the funniest people I've ever met."

"Maybe, but you don't like him in THAT way."

"No."

"Milo though... you know, I'm going to try out for the orchestra. I like hanging out with you and Milo. You are so lucky to have him."

"Have him? I can barely speak when I'm near him. It hasn't improved that much."

"Okay, so maybe we leave boyfriends until Year 9. In the meantime, let's just work on not giggling like little kids when we have to talk to a boy."

"Deal."

"And you know, everything will be okay with your parents, you know. It isn't like they are divorcing you. Just each other."

"I guess I know that, but sometimes it feels that way."

"Just remember that you can always talk to me about it. I'll always be there for you."

"I know, Frances. And me for you. We are absolutely without doubt the most fabulous twelve-year-olds in history. Catch this…" and Ginger chucked a Malteser towards Frances which missed by about a metre.

# July

*Dear Dave and Annabel,*

*I have decided to forgive you for being idiot adults. It is not your fault. Science reveals that your brains are full of information like how long to cook chicken for and how to set up a bank account. It is no wonder that you have no time to have any sense.*

*I realise that you are not getting back together and that you have found new people to annoy. I hope that works out well. If it doesn't, please try to be brave about it.*

*If you have any more feelings of guilt about how much you have made my life difficult over the last year, I am willing to accept your apology by way of a new summer wardrobe of clothes. I realise that you have been very busy being stupid but have you noticed that I am now taller than Mum and have size 8 feet?*

*I will accept cash or vouchers.*

*Lots of love,*

*Ginger xoxo*

The atmosphere at Atherton Academy had changed. There was something different about Year 7. In some cases it was for the worst. Some pupils had found enough loop-holes in the school rules to break them with confidence. In some lessons, a kid would get sent to isolation for troublesome behaviour like having their phone out or sending notes. Twelve-year-olds everywhere were walking around with a swagger in their step, acting like shrunken rappers and saying things like 'wagwan' and 'man'.

In some cases it was definitely for the better. The teachers were beginning to smile weary smiles and talk about their plans for the summer holidays which they seemed obsessed with. Mrs Masterson had told them that she was taking her family to Greece where she wouldn't be doing anything useful except getting a tan and drinking something called ouzo (which sounded fairly gross). Of course, there were far too many assessments going on and Ginger was developing a series of blisters on her thumb from all the writing she was doing. She went out and bought a few new pens from Paperchase to make it more tolerable.

She knew that this summer would be different. There was no long drive to France planned. Instead, she was going to have a week in Cornwall with Mum. Just the two of them. Mum had promised that they would learn to surf. Ginger thought that would be interesting. Later in August, Dad was taking her, Adam and Alex to Majorca for a week. With Sonia. It might have sounded like hell but Ginger was just relieved to be having the kind of holiday her friends had. One with airports and water parks and some actual fun. It would be cool, whatever, with Alex.

There was still quite a lot of term to go though and certain events on the school calendar were filling Ginger and her less sporty friends with dread.

"I swear down, if they make me take part in sports day I will literally die," Tom confessed as they were heading across the forum to Science. "I am more allergic to PE than peanuts and you should see what happens if I eat them."

"Oh, I KNOW!" agreed Frances. "Thank God for the orchestra. Mr Arnold says we'll be too busy playing to compete. He is taking this very seriously."

The plan was that to open Sports Day, the Atherton Academy Orchestra would play the theme from something called 'Chariots of Fire' which currently sounded more like 'Parrots on Fire'. The winners ceremony at the end would be marked with a rendition of the school anthem, a tune from some 90s pop group called Proud which made Ginger feel as though she needed to stick her own head in the toilet and flush it.

However, Ginger agreed that it was better than doing javelin or the 200 metres in front of thirteen hundred pointing pupils. Just.

"If only I had had the good sense to take up the flute instead of spending all my time learning the songs from *Mamma Mia*," sighed Tom as they got to the classroom.

A letter had gone home to inform parents of the various events and ceremonies that they could, if they wished, join the school in celebrating. Ginger had hidden hers beneath her PE kit which was a stupid place to put something as she always forgot to empty the bag herself and left Mum to do it. Mum had immediately phoned her Dad and they had agreed that they would try to get to at least one event together, showing a united front.

Frankly, it was the first time that Sports Day hadn't made Ginger want to fall ill with a temporary but very visibly terrible disease.

Ever since the time she had been forced to wear her yellow 'Sunday' knickers to play rounders at primary school, Ginger had dreaded PE lessons.

Even at Atherton, where the core sports programme was 'varied and challenging for all levels including state-of-the-art gym equipment', PE held a place in Ginger's heart somewhere between sequinned hot pants from Primark and liver.

Most of the girls who hated sport were small and a bit plump and, miraculously, had their periods every week. They were punished for their blatant lies by being forced to walk around the sports track whilst everyone else got on with clubbing each other with hockey sticks or smacking each other in the face during bench-ball. Ginger, on the other hand, looked like someone who might be able to at least chuck a netball through a hoop or run long galloping strides in a cross country race. However, she had no plan to do either. Her PE teacher, Miss Spencer, had insisted in her school report that she try out for both teams. Unable to find a way of hiding her PE report amongst the other good stuff she had wanted Mum to read, Mum had seen the recommendation and demanded that she try out for each team. Furthermore, she'd made it clear that she would not be writing notes for to get out of physical activity ever again.

Ginger was backed into a corner.

Mum had forced her to have to lie.

It was the only way.

In fact, her Mum had believed that for the last four months she had been going to training after school on Mondays and Wednesday when in fact she was either wandering around town with Frances or sitting in Tom's bedroom watching *Home and Away*.

Mum had never enquired about fixtures as she was too busy with Robin, work or getting divorced.

When she was little, it had upset Ginger that her parents worked and that they could hardly ever make a school event. But as she had got older, it was a great relief. These days nothing good ever came from her parents being anywhere near teachers or, in fact, her friends. Especially since they had both started dressing like they were in their late twenties. She thought back affectionately to the days when Dad wore cut-off jeans and a vest rather than skinny jeans and a low-cut t-shirt.

If ever her Mum found out that she wasn't going to sports clubs then she would be in big trouble. Mum said that contact sport was good for her brain and said she was looking forward to meeting Miss Spencer at parent's evening next year to find out how Ginger was doing.

It was good for Ginger's brain in that she had to make

up all sorts of clever stories about what they had been doing in training or how she'd won the match with a leftfield goal in the last minute.

Really, it had been the one successful scheme of the entire year.

On the big day, the entire school was shipped out on special buses to a local athletics track. It was superior to their own facilities in that it had towering rows of stands where everyone could get a good view of the action. Behind the stadium sat towering blocks of flats where people lived in Trevor-like conditions, probably cheered up enormously by the massive school parties who threw themselves around what was basically their garden area.

The weather was also perfect with wisps of fluffy whiteness in a pale blue sky and nothing more. From the stands the view was perfect. Perfect, of course, if your idea of fun was watching teenagers sweat and suffer. Sports Day was one of the big events for school house system. Before they had even arrived the previous September, Ginger had been placed in Gryffindor along with Frances, Tom and Milo whilst poor Stephanie and her lot were allocated to the Slytherin house.

This wasn't *strictly* true but Ginger's house did wear a dark-red stripe in their ties. They were less imaginatively called 'Kestrel'.

Stephanie's house were called 'Kite' and even though there was nothing obviously evil in their title, you could spot a Kite from a mile off. The other two houses were called 'Eagle' and 'Hawk'.

Ginger wondered how they made the decision about who should go in what house and whether there was a similar system to using a magic hat but perhaps with some other magic thing. Possibly they had a team of birds of prey who pecked at photos.

Where DID teachers come up with these lunatic ideas?

The stands were divided up between each house with athletes at the front wearing t-shirts that corresponded with house colour. Behind the athletes sat the non-competitors who were to be treated throughout like freaks of nature. Roughly speaking, there was a row of school-nerds with their Minecraft games on hand held-devices, a row of pupils who were physical misfits for one reason or another, then a row of pupils who smoked too heavily to run more than a metre.

One small section had been reserved for parents and it was only then that she realised that she hadn't discussed it with Mum. It was quite a surprise to see Dad and Sonia plus Mum and Robin there. Reassuringly, all of them appeared to be engrossed in the silly things they were always engrossed in on their phones. Dad was probably reading a Twitter feed about Norwich City Football Club; Mum was inevitably checking to see if she'd won a bid on a useless eBay item that she'd put in the cupboard. Robin and Sonia were probably communicating with each other about how daft they'd been to wind up with these two nutcases.

It seemed pretty mean to put these tribes together, thought Ginger, as it was clear that throughout the event the back row would make the lives of the other two rows hell.

Perhaps that was a cunning plan to persuade them to compete the following year. Clever!

Ginger however felt pretty good as she followed Milo, Frances and Mr Arnold plus about another twenty musicians down the steps to where they would be playing. Ginger managed to only hit two or three members of Kite with the wide end of her instrument.

Milo was dressed in an athlete's t-shirt because he had insisted that he both wanted to perform and compete, something that made Mr Arnold look puzzled. He said that this had never happened before. Nobody who went to orchestra could run for toffee. Milo had insisted though and sure enough, his name was down on the Year 7 boys' 100 metres and discus.

Mr Arnold looked a little nervous about the performance and kept putting something in his mouth that Ginger thought was probably some kind of anxiety medicine. If the pupils of Atherton had been allowed to gamble, they would have all put bets on him being the teacher most likely to have a nervous breakdown before the end of term. His sweat patches had grown from the size of Ireland to the size of Russia in the last ten minutes.

"It'll be fine, Sir. We're all ready and even if we're not, nobody will be listening!" she cheerfully pointed out.

The band were placed on a structure that raised them about fifty centimetres off the ground. They were in front of the field events but behind the running track. Facing the bleacher seating, they were also positioned at around the fifty metre point of where the 100 metres runners would sprint by.

On four, the band began to play. The effect was hard to interpret as the noise from the crowds was still far too loud for anyone to be able to hear whether Hermione was in time or how lovely Milo's lead was.

Ginger began to enjoy herself.

The only person who even came close to the orchestra was Miss Spencer, the PE teacher, who mouthed 'bravo' repeatedly and clapped in a very uncool way.

As she played, Ginger looked out across the scene in front of her.

Miss Spencer was attracted to the stands where her house, Eagle, seemed to be engaged in the unwholesome activity of shouting rude things at girls who ran past without bras under their team t-shirts. Their attention was then cruelly directed towards an awkward looking Year 7 girl who was apparently carrying six troll dolls in her arms as she entered the field for the javelin. Brittany! Ginger wondered how Brittany had survived an entire year. Looking at her placing the dolls in a small circle on the floor by her feet, Ginger guessed that Brittany just didn't give a damn about what anyone thought of her.

There was a lot they could all learn from the Brittanys of this world.

Oblivious, she continued to chat to her toys whilst screams of derision came from the stands. This was particularly embarrassing for the school as the parents in the stands were directly above the shouting older boys and could hear it all.

The orchestra was entirely drowned out by the rumpus so it didn't matter if Hermione hit the wrong note or when Frances lost her place and started playing the opening again.

The spectacle of Sports Day played out as it had in English schools for decades. Ginger had seen it on CBBC enough times. There were the boys who lived for sport. Their trainers were expensive and they had muscles. These boys did things like hold their hands up to give each other high-fives. They grunted when they threw things. They punched the air when they won a race. Then there were the really athletic girls who seemed to work so hard that Ginger felt a blush of admiration as they tried their best and often succeeded. One girl was famous across the school for winning a place on junior Team GB. *Perhaps that would be cool,* she thought. Of course, there were the pupils who had been entered for an event through no fault of their own and looked as though they would rather be anywhere else, perhaps at Camp Green Lake digging holes. Their faces just looked permanently puzzled. Perhaps she was not the only alien at Atherton.

When they finished their first rendition of 'Chariots of Fire', they put down their bows and relaxed, relishing the fact that they could enjoy a prime position and the breeze. For what felt like hours, Ginger was able to sit in the sunshine and chat to Frances. They talked about the summer, all the events of the year and even about Ginger's parents' break-up. Frances confided in Ginger that her older sister was pregnant and that her Mum was furious. As they talked, Frances picked at a recent injury that had formed a large scab on her knee but Ginger didn't mind. Everyone had their own way of dealing with life's challenges.

A lot of the time they weren't paying attention and certainly hadn't noticed Mum and Miss Spencer appear at the side of the plinth where the orchestra were seated. They approached Mr Arnold first. Then, Mr Arnold was waving his arms around and looking quite cross as he argued with the two women. Ginger felt her stomach in her toes as she contemplated what was on earth was going on. It couldn't be good. It never was.

Mum broke free from the argument and climbed up on the stage, hitching up her skirt so that she didn't trip and was all of a sudden in Ginger's face.

"So, young lady, or should I say star of the netball and bench-ball team. I've just been hearing about what an important member of the team you've been this year."

All around her, band geeks stared.

"All that energy you have saved doing God only knows what needs to be used up and so I've just entered you for the 100 metres. A place came up when some other girl accidentally dropped her bed on her foot when she was getting out of it and there is nobody else. You are going to run so go get into position. NOW!"

Miss Spencer was behind Mum nodding her head furiously as if this was the best news she had heard in her entire life.

The embarrassment was perhaps the worst of the entire year and Ginger wished that the Eagles would start a chant directed at some poor, over-weight Year 8 boy again.

Mum and Miss Spencer were now back in conversation about how teenagers were under the influence of TV reality shows and didn't do half enough exercise. They were away in the grown-up world in that way adults sometimes do, completely oblivious to the young people around them who might be going into cardiac arrest for all they knew. Mostly, Len Goodman and Mylie Cyrus were to blame, it seemed.

Frances turned to Ginger whilst this was going on and told her she had an idea.

"Look at my knee, Ginger," she whispered.

"Yes, it's disgusting. So what?"

"There is blood."

The next thing Ginger knew, Franny had grabbed her cello bow and thrown it onto the floor.

"Bend down to pick it up!" ordered Frances, through gritted teeth.

As Ginger bent down, Frances grabbed her head and pushed it further. With the other hand she wiped as much blood as she could from the wound onto Ginger's face. When Ginger lifted her head back into the day light, she looked as though she had broken her nose. "Perfect", said Frances.

"Erm, Miss Spencer, I don't think Ginger can..."

Ginger silently scolded herself for what she was doing but decided that the guilt was something she could manage if it were to mean that she wouldn't have to do the 100 metres in her school uniform. She shot Frances a glance of thanks and wondered if anyone had ever had a better best friend?

"What have you done?" screamed Mum, accusingly and with not the least hint of sympathy for what looked to be her daughter's bleeding nose.

"I think I just broke it... erm... on Frances's erm... chair, when I bent down."

"I don't' believe it!" shouted Mum.

Frances even managed to churn out some tears but inconspicuously covered her knee with her instrument to avoid the women discovering the source of the blood.

"I'm afraid I can't run, Mum..." Ginger cried, thinking about how sad she would be if Trevor were ever to go to Hamster heaven and conjuring up some tears.

From that moment on, Mum became gentler and insisted that Ginger accompany her to the stands where they would go and ask Robin or Dad to drive them to the Emergency department at the hospital. She even hunted in her handbag for a bundle of tissues to wipe up the blood.

Ginger made sure that she didn't reveal too much of her nose and squealed when Miss Spencer tried to examine her.

"Let's go," she said softly. "Mr Arnold can take care of the cello."

Before long, Ginger was eating ice-cream in bed and listening to Trevor run maniacally around her wheel. *Thanks, Trevor*, she thought. *You got me out of a pickle*.

At the hospital, Ginger had immediately been found out by a kindly nurse. The nurse had told Mum, Robin, Dad and Sonia to leave the examination room as Ginger was a big girl and it would all be okay.

As soon as they had been ushered out, Ginger remembered that there was nothing wrong with her nose whatsoever and that she was fifty seconds away from being discovered.

Ginger was forced to confide in the nurse.

"Look, although I do not approve of anyone wasting the time of the NHS, I do feel your pain. Look at these legs, do they look like the legs of an athlete?"

The nurse pointed down to legs that were unusually stumpy and probably not meant for sport.

"Where did you get the blood?"

"My friend's scab," confessed Ginger, half-smiling but still ashamed of herself.

"Well if you ever pull a stunt like this again on my shift, I WILL rat you out. But this time, we'll just say that it is a little bruised and that there's nothing to worry about. I suppose you'd like me to put a plaster on it for effect, eh?"

Ginger had nodded sheepishly and kept perfectly still as he fake-fixed-up her face.

As she was leaving the cubicle, she turned to the nurse and told him with pride that it hadn't been her idea, but her friend Frances'.

"She's a genius," she told him and he laughed.

In the car park, she was left waiting in Robin's car as the two couples talked. Ginger could see that the shared experience of Ginger's accident was doing wonders for international relations. Mum and Sonia were smiling as they talked and everyone seemed to have forgotten about Ginger, which was exactly how she liked it for now. An easy life, adults being selfish and thinking of nothing but themselves. Much better than trying to work out how their daughter had become a psychopath or why she would tell elaborate lies to get out of being on a sports team.

Before long, it was the last day of term. The end of the school year was marked with a celebration assembly including the distribution of various certificates and medals. The school rewarded pupils for effort, progress and attendance.

The heat in the theatre was stifling. Nobody had thought to open the windows and Ginger could feel her shirt sticking to her damp back. She could literally feel springs of hair pinging out of her plait, desperate to party in the humidity.

For once, Ginger had managed to sit next to both Frances and Tom, and Milo was only a couple of rows away, fiddling with a key chain that he somehow got away with wearing. Ginger wondered how he managed to get away with his heavy metal when she wasn't even allowed to wear more than one friendship bracelet.

Brittany was sitting next to Hermione up above them. They looked like they were enjoying each other's company and she wondered what they were talking about? Elves and pixies?

Frances held her hand as each award was read out and looked nervous under her luscious dark fringe. It felt good to have her there, along with the new friends they had made. The battle scars of the year felt as though they were healing and Ginger thought that however hard life got, however many swerve Maltesers were thrown at you, if you had a friendship like theirs, anything was possible.

Ginger was more than happy with two progress awards and didn't mind in the slightest that she was passed over for a Contribution to Sports Merit.

Taking to the stage to receive her certificate, Ginger looked out at the audience and wondered what their years had been like.

Had they suffered a little bit too? Was anyone out there thinking 'oh, I so wish that every day was a school day?' Had everyone felt a humiliation or disappointment? Had everyone experienced some act of meanness, some act of cruelty from another kid? Did everyone out there wish that their hair was a little less greasy, curly or straight?

Ginger knew that she would never know. But she *could* make an educated guess.

Returning to her seat, she saw Tom receive a special merit for his part in the school play and Frances get 100% full attendance just as she had every year since reception. Ginger nearly clapped her hands off with pride.

Of all the Year 7s, Milo was clearly the runaway success story and Ginger worried that his feet would be getting tired from being on his feet so much. A small rain forest had died making his certificates.

She only felt a little jealous.

Mostly, she felt really lucky to be his friend.

Were they friends? She thought they probably were. There couldn't be that many people that you met in life who not only saved you from a drunken teenage hooligan but also got you out of trouble with the police.

Soon, Ginger's mind wandered to the summer holidays and she was just picturing herself in a very tasteful swimsuit when she was alerted to the ever infuriating babyish whine of Stephanie who was sitting on the row in front. Yes, she and Stephanie had come a long way since September's den-making, the drawings and the accidental internet campaign, but something in Steph's gleaming eye caught Ginger's attention.

Stephanie was looking at Ginger as she winked and told Lydia that Milo Costigan would be her boyfriend by Christmas.

But that would be another catastrophic adventure in the life of Ginger Mclean.

Printed in July 2019
by Rotomail Italia S.p.A., Vignate (MI) - Italy